What family
does she belong to?
Or is she a princess
from some country
attending incognito?

CONTENTS

USING
POTIONS!

MUNCH MUNCH

I Shall Survive Using Potions! Volume 1
by FUNA

Translated by Garrison Denim
Edited by CHaSE

Copyright © 2017 FUNA
Illustrations by Sukima

First published in Japan in 2017 by Kodansha Ltd., Tokyo.
Publication rights for this English edition arranged through Kodansha Ltd., Tokyo.

Find more books like this one at www.j-novel.club!

President and Publisher: Samuel Pinansky
Managing Editor: Aimee Zink

ISBN: 978-1-7183-7190-3
Printed in Korea
First Printing: August 2020
10 9 8 7 6 5 4 3 2 1

I SHALL SURVIVE USING POTIONS!

1

Author: FUNA
Illustrator: Sukima

Chapter 1:
I'd Like Some Perks for My Reincarnation, Please!

Kaoru Nagase, twenty-two years old.

An office lady with silky black hair that came down to her shoulder blades, who stood at 158 centimeters tall (perfectly appropriate for her age) and always had a slightly—okay, a REALLY harsh look in her eyes. She'd graduated with a degree in science from a national university and found a job at a medium-sized company back in her hometown. It'd been half a year since she started her convenient life of commuting from home to her job, much to the joy of her parents, while she saved up money.

She had a family of five, consisting of her parents, a brother two years older than her, and a sister who was three years younger. They all got along well, though her little sister Yuki seemed a bit disappointed at not gaining complete control over the room they shared even after Kaoru found a job.

She'd finally gotten used to her work and was coming back home after finishing an hour and a half's worth of overtime. Despite this, and without warning, Kaoru felt like she was about to lose consciousness, stopping where she stood.

Not good, not good… If I fall over and hit my head or something, I'm done for. Falling over would be bad, so I'm just gonna crouch down slowly…

But even without crouching down, the feeling of dizziness had passed in an instant. Just as Kaoru turned forward to start walking again, thinking it was a slight bout of vertigo caused by low blood pressure or something, she froze in place.

"What...*is* this...?"

The area in front of her—no, everything around her was completely white. An area devoid of anything else spread out before her. As she was frozen in place and unable to comprehend what was going on, a voice came from behind her:

"You must be Kaoru Nagase, right?"

Surprised, Kaoru turned around to find a man who appeared to be in his mid-twenties. He had golden hair and blue eyes, and was sort of like the physical embodiment of what every woman would consider to be a "good man." He wore a white outfit that seemed like something an aristocrat from ancient Rome would wear, with a gentle smile spreading across his face.

Uh-oh, this doesn't look good...

Kaoru was a fan of light novels, so she had a feeling she knew where this was going. The man introduced himself as "someone in charge of watching over this world," like she'd been expecting him to. Put simply, it was like he was what humans would call "God," or at least something close to it.

According to "God" here, this whole incident was supposedly the result of some sort of accident. The world as we know it actually exists along multiple space-time continuums (basically parallel worlds) as part of a "multiverse." These parallel worlds usually exist without interference from each other, but every once in a while a space-time anomaly or energy deviation or the like causes different space-times to approach and affect each other. If these events take the form of small holes or cracks in the space-time continuum, then they can be taken care of by dealing with the problem ASAP. At worst, however, these events might end up involving multiple worlds, and turn into a disaster of epic proportions.

To protect against such events, there existed a race of beings beyond humanity's wildest imagination, beings who were so far advanced that they could only be called "Gods." These beings watched over the worlds and adjusted the balance of space-time as necessary. Because of that, any anomalies or deviations were spotted in a timely manner, then dispersed and taken care of before the anomalies could reach disaster levels.

The incident this time was a result of this man going to disperse a small anomaly, just as he always did; unluckily for Kaoru, she'd gotten caught up in it as well. Her physical body had taken heavy damage, and though God had rushed to recover her consciousness and soul, Kaoru was already considered dead back on Earth.

"I'm sorry, I'm so terribly sorry! I've never made a mistake like this in all my thousands of years doing this..."

The man who claimed to be God appeared to be truly sorry as he bowed his head and apologized in earnest. A bitter smile crossed Kaoru's face, as if to say these sorts of things just happened.

"I mean, you know, it's fine... Well, no, it's not, but there's no way around it now, right? You just made a little mistake when doing your job of watching over the world. I guess I had a bit of bad luck this time too, that's all."

With a light laugh, Kaoru explained how it didn't hurt and that she hadn't suffered when it happened. All humans had to die eventually. But God had a pained expression on his face.

"I'm humbled to hear you say that... However, as the supervisor for this world, it's evident that I must take measures to aid you. As luck would have it, I succeeded in preserving your consciousness and soul, so it's possible to have you live a new life through the reconstruction of your physical body."

"Wait, you can bring me back to life? Like, back to the same life I had before?" Kaoru asked him out of surprise.

But God shook his head regretfully. "I'm sorry... Your physical body has already been declared deceased and, erm...taken care of... This world is very finely tuned, so if I were to use my powers to forcefully intervene, there's a chance its balance would collapse and cause a massive distortion."

Aw man... So that means there's no place for me there anymore... If I tried forcing my way back in, then I'd just be causing trouble for everyone.

Kaoru had quickly come to terms with the situation she'd been placed in.

"My recommendation would be to start a new life in a different world. Even if we were to use a bit of excessive force on a world that hasn't progressed as far, nothing much would change. And, luckily enough, there's one such unadjusted world that's quite similar to Earth... It's likely that the same world split off at some point in the distant past due to a massive spatial distortion. My guess is that this resulted in a substantial migration of flora and fauna between the two, likely on a continental scale, and, as a result, the people, plants, and animals generally appear to be the same. The civilization there is far behind that of Earth, something akin to medieval Europe, but it's a world where you could still live comfortably as a human."

God seemed desperate to send Kaoru off to another world. On top of there being no better way to go about this, it seemed he wanted to atone for his mistake and make it up to Kaoru, so of course he would be desperate...

Understanding this, Kaoru resigned herself and agreed.

"I understand. It doesn't seem like there are any other good ideas besides that, so I'll take you up on your offer."

"Oh, thank you! Then I'll start the preparations right—"

"Ah, hold on a second!"

Though he seemed relieved and in a rush to start the preparations, Kaoru managed to reign God back in.

"The medieval world is far more dangerous than the modern world, right? Injuries, disease, crime, wars—those sorts of things would be more rampant. I don't think a girl who doesn't have a clue what's going on, being thrust into the middle of all that by herself, would be able to scrape by. Like, at all. At best, I would end up as a slave or in a brothel. At worst, I could be dead the same day I arrive..."

"..."

A bead of sweat ran down God's temple to his cheek. Kaoru couldn't imagine his body having been built with such a bodily function, so he was most likely doing it on purpose to show some sort of psychological reaction. That was some real attention to detail.

"Because of that..." Kaoru stuck her pointer finger right at God. "I'd like to request some sort of cheat powers!"

"Ch-Cheat...powers...?" He didn't seem to have a clue what was going on.

"That's right, cheat powers! If a girl like me, who won't know left from right, is going to live in this new world by herself, she's going to need some special abilities, don't you think? Oh! I'll need to be able to understand the language and writing system over there as well. And since it'll be a more uncivilized world, I guess the age women can get married at would be a lot lower too. So if you don't make me a bit younger, I don't think I'll be able to live a happy life, you know...?"

Kaoru's life was on the line here, so she was going to take this opportunity to go all in.

"Y-Yes... I don't completely understand...but very well. Reconstruction of your physical body and granting you powers falls under the authority of whoever is the supervisor for that world, so I'll be sure to request they take care of you beforehand. You can talk over the details with them once you arrive."

"Please and thank you! Oh, and there are two favors I'd like to ask while I'm still here. Is that all right?"

God nodded, agreeing to Kaoru's request. "As long as they don't lead to any problems, then yes, anything you like. You have that right, after all."

"In that case... First, as long as it doesn't make me appear too different from the other humans in this new world, I want to take the body I have now—or, well, the body I had—and make it younger. I never got a chance to repay my parents back on Earth, so I was thinking I'd like to do that now by leaving their genes in this new world. Though, that's only if I manage to get married and leave grandchildren for them..."

While Kaoru laughed, God's eyes were wide open, as if this came as a complete shock to him.

"My other request is that I'd like to say goodbye to my family and friends. Since I died an unnatural death, I feel like that might leave some emotional scars... That's why I want to let them know I'm all right, and to see them off with a smile. Oh, I'm not asking for something absurd like meeting with them in person, of course. If I could have a minute or two to talk to them in their dreams, then that'd be enough. Even if they think it's not real and it's all just a dream, I'd be happy if I could make them feel even a little more at ease..."

God nodded in assent, promising to grant her requests.

"Then just as you asked, I will connect you to everyone's dreams: one with your family, and the other with your two friends. It's been ten days since the incident back on Earth, so please, take care not to leave any regrets behind. As soon as that's over, I will transfer you to the new world. Once you arrive there, I will no longer be able to take any direct part in what happens, but I'll be sure to tell the supervisor there to take care of you. I'm truly, truly sorry about all this. Now, may you have a good life!"

With those words, God saw Kaoru off with an amiable smile.

It's only been ten days since then...

Koichi lay in bed, thinking about his little sister, who'd just passed away the other day.

The middle child of three siblings... It'd been half a year since she graduated from college. She loved to read, was knowledgeable in many things, and could be a bit of a tomboy. Though she looked like a cute girl, she always had this intense look in her eyes. She was more of a little brother to him, making it feel like he had both a little brother and a little sister instead of just two sisters.

He'd recently been laughing and joking with her as she retold her "incredible tales of valor" about her time at school and in the workplace, and he never thought she'd go off and die sooner than their parents. Not to mention she'd died a mysterious and unnatural death, where her body basically exploded in front of a bunch of witnesses while she was on her way back home. This caused an uproar, of course. People thought it could have been anything—ultra-small explosives, a murder caused by stringing up piano wires, yōkai, or even the work of the devil. The insensitive mass media jumped on the unusual story, with a cult even trying to use it to scam people out of money, and so on and so forth...

Things had finally settled down a little, but it'd be a long time before they settled down for good. Koichi had kept himself distracted, because he'd been so busy, but now that he had some time to himself, the sadness was beginning to close in.

His parents and Yuki were probably going through the same thing. Even though they'd all gone to bed early, he kept hearing the sound of the toilet flushing or the refrigerator door being opened and closed. But now, everything was finally quiet.

Tears ran down his cheeks as he thought about his little sister. A flood of different emotions washed over him. Maybe it was because of his continuous lack of sleep over the past few days, but, before he knew it, he'd fallen into a deep sleep...

"Aha, you're here! You took forever to go to sleep, Koichi!"

Oh, a lucid dream...

I was sitting around a table with the other four members of my family. Looking at me with a smile on her face was my little sister, who should have no longer been with us. Though it had only been a mere ten days, I was overcome with a sense of sadness and longing.

"Let me get right to explaining now that everyone's here. Basically, I died because God made a mistake, and, as an apology, he's going to send me to another world with cheat powers!"

"What the hell kinda light novel is that supposed to be?!"

I couldn't help but butt in with a sudden retort. Wait, this was my dream, so the lack of imagination would actually be my own fault. That was kinda sad, me.

"Did you make sure to have him take responsibility for what he did, Kaoru? You make sure to get him to compensate you!"

I smacked my head on the table at my mom's stupid joke... Wait, why did it hurt?

"It's all right, I made sure to have him promise me cheat powers, and some other stuff too! I'm getting resurrected in my own body, and I'm getting my youth back as well. I'm gonna make so many descendants for the Nagase household in this other world! Our family genes are gonna run rampant there!"

"Well, well, ain't that somethin'... Then it looks like you'll be competin' with Yuki and Koichi here!"

Dad was almost as bad as Mom... No, maybe he was a bit worse.

"Hey, Sis, could you send a hot prince or some super-expensive diamond back to our world?"

Oh my god, Yuki...

"Sorry, it doesn't seem like I can swing that. Ah, it's almost time... All right, everyone, be good! I'm gonna be doing my best in my new world as well! Oh, and since I'm getting cheat powers, I can use them to keep myself safe and make some easy money! I'm pretty much guaranteed a stable future, so don't worry about me, all right? Welp... Dad, Mom, Big Bro, Yuki... Take care, everyone! Thank you for everything, and goodbye!"

"Take care now!"

"I hope you'll be happy!"

"Get yourself a good man, Big Sis!"

"...You know what to do, right, Kaoru? Keep information about yourself a secret, and keep yourself safe!"

"I got it, I got it! See ya!"

Morning... Haha, was I stupid or something? Why would I tell her that? As if Kaoru wouldn't know something as basic as that... *Wait, am I stupid?!* That was my dream, so why was I reacting to it like that? You know what, I should just go ahead and grab some breakfast.

Getting out of bed, I headed straight down to the first floor. Everyone in our family wore pajamas to breakfast. We didn't have to worry if we spilled food on them, and since we would go to the bathroom and brush our teeth afterward, we could avoid splattering our work clothes with toothpaste or getting them wrinkled. Very logical, if I say so myself.

Dad and Yuki were already sitting at the table, so I sat down in my seat as well. They were already downing some miso soup, and Mom was still getting the plates of grilled salmon ready for them. But something about everyone seemed a bit off. They were fidgeting around, sneaking peeks at each other's faces. It was an indescribable feeling of restlessness. What was the matter with them...?

For some reason, at that time, part of the conversation from my dream crossed my mind.

"Our family's genes are gonna run rampant there!"

"Is our family a bunch of mice or cockroaches or something?!" I blurted out suddenly. What the heck was I even saying?!

PBFTTTTTT!!!

Miso soup suddenly came spurting out of Dad's and Yuki's mouths and noses. Ah, yes, our family's habit of wearing pajamas to breakfast had been proven practical!

"Good grief, how nasty—OW, hot!!!"

Behind me, Mom was picking up a plate she had dropped. *Aw man, my grilled salmon...*

"Cheat powers in another world..." Dad murmured.

"A hot prince and a super-expensive diamond..."

"She told you that wasn't going to happen..." Mom retorted to my sister's mumbling.

...Silence. A hush fell over the room. Then...

"...Haha..."

"…Ahaha…"

"Ahahahahahaha!"

We laughed. The four of us laughed and laughed, and kept on laughing. Streams of water ran down our cheeks, but we paid them no mind and kept laughing. All of us were late for school and work that day.

"Hey, you're here!"

There were two girls sitting around the small table in front of me.

Oh, a dream, huh…

One of the girls here was my close friend who had passed away ten days ago, the other being a close friend I had known since middle school—and who was now my only close friend left. I had cried my eyes out every day since Kaoru's accident, but I'd finally been able to calm down a little. Maybe it was because I was still lingering on what had happened, or maybe it was because I'd managed to sort out my feelings, but now I was beginning to see her in my dreams…

"I'm sorry for dying so soon, Kyo-chan. There was more I wanted to do as the three of us… I'm really sorry."

Unable to hold myself back anymore, I threw myself around Kaoru's slender body, tears streaming down my face.

"You stupid! Dumb! Dummy! Why did you have to go and die like that?! You big! Stupid! Idiot!!!" I kept crying my eyes out.

"Calm down, Kyoko. It wasn't like Kaoru wanted to die. It doesn't seem like we have much time, so let's just listen to what she has to say."

Reiko was acting like she usually did, always keeping her cool… Though this was my dream, so that was probably only because that was the type of person I saw her as.

Well, that aside, I finally had a chance to talk to Kaoru, even if it was only in a dream. I'd probably never get another opportunity to meet with her in a dream as vivid as this.

"Kaoru…"

"I'm sorry. It seems like the reason I died was because God kinda screwed up…"

"Huh? Then they can bring you back to life!"

"Yeah, they can…but not in this world, though. They said they were going to bring me back to life in another one, some place that's kinda like medieval Europe."

"Why?! Why can't you come back to this world?! Why not…?!"

Reiko got up and patted me gently on the back, but I couldn't stop sobbing.

"Ah, sorry girls, I don't really have that much time… Anyway, I died because God made a mistake, but he's going to revive me in another world with all my memories intact, so I plan on living a happy life there. Thanks for always being with me since middle school, I'll never forget you two. Be happy!"

"Kaoru? Kaoru! Kaoruuuuuuu!"

"Do you have anything you want to tell your family, Kaoru?" Even in my dreams, Reiko kept herself calm and collected.

"Oh, it's all good. I already made sure to say my goodbyes to them. See ya, you two, and farewell!"

Kaoru vanished into thin air, leaving only Reiko and I behind. After making sure that I had finally stopped crying first, Reiko burst into tears herself.

"Ahh… Aaaaaahhhhhh!" She bawled her eyes out as she clung to me. "Waaaaaaaaaaaaah!"

As I watched Reiko cry, I finally understood. She was just that type of girl, always holding herself back, putting others before herself…

"I'm sorry, Reiko… Even though I knew we didn't have much time, I went and wasted it… Even though this should have been valuable time for you to talk with Kaoru more…"

I held Reiko tight, and the two of us just kept on crying…

…Morning. My alarm clock was ringing at the usual time, waking me up just like always. As I got up, I noticed my pillow was soaking wet with a mixture of tears, drool, and snot. Even in my dreams, Kaoru was Kaoru, and Reiko was Reiko. My best friends…

Then my phone began ringing on the side table next to my bed. My closest friends knew I would wake up at 5 a.m. on the dot on weekdays, and if they needed to get hold of me first thing in the morning, they would call between 5 and 5:01 a.m. Anytime after that and I'd be busy going to the bathroom, washing my face, or cooking or something. It wasn't like anyone would call me that early more than a few times a year anyway. Today just happened to be one of those few times. But who could it be this early in the morning?

Reaching for my phone, I had a feeling I knew who it was. Even though I thought it couldn't be possible, part of me was still half-convinced I was right.

Picking up my phone, I pressed the call button and placed it against my ear.

"Hey… Yeah. Huh? Settle things with God? How though? Wait, punch them? Like, but how? No, I'm totally on board! Do you wanna go to a shrine and kick around their donation box? Yeah? Got it. We'll head over to Kaoru's place for a bit of information gathering then. Yeah, sounds good! See you Saturday!"

Pressing the end call button on my phone, I sat myself down on my bed.

Heh…

My face broke into a grin.

Ehe, eheheh. Eheheheheh…

I hugged my pillow tight. *Eugh, it's all sticky…*

Kaoru didn't tell her friends about the whole "being younger again" thing. Somehow, just imagining what their reactions would be like was a terrifying prospect for her…

Chapter 2: Potions

The next thing I noticed, I was in a white space. This was the second time it had happened, so I was kinda getting used to it now. Turning around, I found myself face-to-face with a cute girl with blonde hair and blue eyes who looked around fifteen to sixteen years old. She froze on the spot, a look of surprise on her face.

…*Jackpot.*

Wait, what did I even think I won in the first place?!

"Are you the goddess in charge of this world?"

After I asked, the girl who looked like a goddess finally broke free from her stupor, answering gleefully.

"Yes, that's right! I'm Celestine, this world's supervisor. Welcome to Verny! We're happy to have you!"

Well *she* seems pretty excited about all this… I thought it would have been more trouble to have a burden like me pushed onto her…

"Um, I think you've probably already heard from the God in charge of Earth, but I'll be in your debt as of now…"

My future was riding on this, so I had to be humble… Wait, she was a goddess, so of course I would be humble in front of her! Jeez!

"Yes, yes, yes, I've heard! I'm truly grateful to you!"

…Wait, why was she grateful? Shouldn't this be more of a pain in the butt for her? I couldn't see what she was getting at, so I tried asking her directly.

"Um, why would you say that? Shouldn't I be a bit of a nuisance for you?"

"N-No, not at all! I really am grateful!"

After taking the time to listen to the details, I got a rough idea as to why. It seemed like Little Miss Goddess here really put the God in charge of Earth on a pedestal. He seemed to be a pretty famous person... Well, he was a famous "God," even among the other supervisors, and was popular with the other young goddesses.

Wait, so that guy's a friggin' normie!

Well, anyway, though she was ecstatic to be in charge of a world similar to his, whenever they had their "analogous world supervisor get-togethers" (They actually have those?!), she was always left behind by her senior goddesses and didn't have a chance to talk to him directly. She could only stare at him longingly from a distance.

And that's where I came in. Not only had the person—er, God—whom she admired so much come to see her directly, oh no, not only that! He bowed his head and asked for a favor, for her to let him know how I was doing from time to time! To apologize for the trouble, he said to ask him anytime if there was something he could do for her! Oh, what good fortune! Oh, what bliss!!! She was ready to throw in a little extra service for me, it seemed. Well, as long as she was helping me out, I guess that was a good thing...

And so, the two of us got into the nitty-gritty. My life was depending on this, so I was dead serious.

"In any case, the things that God promised me went like this: One cheat power, the ability to communicate, read, and write in any language here, and to bring me back to life in a younger version of my current body. Oh, and is there anything that'd be inconvenient about my old body? Anything that would make me stand out too much, or get me discriminated against, or mean I couldn't have children... Anything like that?"

"Oh, no. Black hair and black eyes are a bit unusual, but it's not like there aren't any people with those traits, and discrimination is practically nonexistent. There are no differences between your body and the bodies of the other people here, so there won't be any problems concerning you having offspring."

All right, that's one load off my shoulders.

"Then let's get to deciding that cheat. A question before that though: Does magic exist in this world? Like, are there monsters here, and people who hunt said monsters as a job?"

This was an extremely vital question. Depending on the answer, it could change what type of cheat I would pick and what sort of life I would try living here.

"I'm not too sure what this 'cheat' is supposed to be, but the other God requested I give you one superior skill that would help you live in this world. Also, everything you just asked about does indeed exist here: magic, monsters, hunters, and the like."

Aw yeah, all according to plan!

"Understood. Then, as for my cheat, I'd like to request the power to create medicine that has any effect I want it to have."

"…Huh?"

Ever since the God back on Earth promised me that I could have a cheat power, I'd been wondering what I should choose. If I could only have one, what should I use it for? For fights? Yeah, right. I was a girl with sticks for arms, so I wouldn't be able to do much with that. Even if I made myself the strongest there was, if I were to get famous because of it, then that'd be the end of me. Game over. Surprise attacks, huge groups of people coming to fight with me, getting poisoned, traps being laid for me, being taken hostage… You name it and it could happen to me.

It would be a similar story if I went for magic. To make matters worse, there could also be people who would want my powers to run through their family's veins. It might be all right if I was married off in some sort of political marriage, but there was the possibility they would just treat me like livestock or something... *Brrr, scary!*

In the end, both those abilities would probably just be used for fighting. I'd like to avoid putting my life on the line every day fighting monsters, and I didn't want to kill people while fighting in foreign wars, so I'd take a hard pass on those skills, thank you very much!

Anyway, I didn't want any special powers that had a chance of being passed down genetically. I was going to do my best to keep my abilities a secret, and even if people did find out about them, I wanted my power to be something that was limited to me and only me. It had to be something that couldn't be used for evil or to hurt anyone, so as to make people think it wasn't worth threatening me or holding me hostage. Above all else, there was no point if it didn't meet my original goal of "an ability that lets me live a safe and happy life."

Question: What was the most dangerous thing in a less civilized world? Monsters? Bandits? Wrong. While they were dangerous in their own ways, they could be avoided as long as you had the cash to do so. You could move to one of the safer areas of a big town, for example, and hire a bunch of guards to protect you.

I wasn't talking about that sort of danger, but one that couldn't be avoided.

I was talking about injury and disease. Illnesses that could easily be solved with a single shot or a surgery in modern Japan would be fatal in this world. The same went for injuries. You could make a complete recovery back in Japan, but living the rest of your life with the after-effects of an injury, especially if the wound got infected, was a no-go here. Being prepared for those things was probably the most crucial thing for me to do.

Another important thing, of course, was being able to make money. It wasn't going to be easy for a young girl like me to save up money in an unfamiliar parallel world, which was why a power I could use to turn a profit would make everything perfect. That was how I came up with the idea of "the ability to create medicine that has any effect I want it to have." That way I wouldn't have to worry about getting sick or injured, and I could open a little potion shop or something and live a life of leisure. Since they would cost me nothing to make, it should be a cinch to save up enough money to live on my own, at least until I could find my spouse-to-be. There were people out there fighting monsters for a living after all, and I wouldn't have to worry about my potions losing to any of my potential business rivals... I mean, I could make potions for free with any effect I wanted them to have. There was no way I could lose. And that was why I'd decided upon "medicine" as my cheat power.

"As I said, I'd like the ability to create any medicine with the effect I want it to have. Since the civilization of this world is far behind compared to that of Earth, diseases and injuries are terrifying to me. I could end up unable to use a hand or leg ever again just because I broke a bone, or die from a sickness that could have been fixed with a single shot back home. It's all the more reason I wanted to make this my request. I'm being sent to this world because God made a mistake and now I can't live on Earth anymore... I'm trying to cover for just a small fraction of that disadvantage with this power, but is that selfish? Would God say no to that, I wonder?"

"…I-It's all right, it's all right! I understand! I was just confirming what kind of ability you wanted, that's all!"

All right! Let's keep this ball rolling!

Breaking eye contact with the goddess, I looked down and pretended to be deep in thought.

"Oh, I guess it'd be pretty inconvenient to not have some kind of container when I create the medicine. What would be good, I wonder… Maybe something small and easy to carry, like mini test tubes or something… Or maybe it'd be better to have them in drinking bottles so I could line them up how I want to in a shop? What should I do about the caps, I wonder? It might be a problem using aluminum because of how this world's civilization isn't too far along, but using corks would mean I'd have to worry about things like leakage or it going stale. What to do, what to do…"

I stole a glance at the goddess. Yup, that was the sort of face that said she had no idea what I was getting at.

"It's all such a hassle…so could I just have it so the medicine appears in whatever container I'm thinking of?"

"Y-Yes, I suppose anything is fine, if it's just for containers…"

Yesss, I got her to give me her word!

"Then that sums up the things God had promised me."

"Is that so? Then let's get started with creating your body."

"Ah, hold on a second, please!"

I reined the goddess back in. I did this to God too, huh…

"I may be able to live a little longer with this, but it certainly seems like I would end up living a life of discomfort at this rate. This place is so far behind compared to Earth, and not exactly safe either…"

"W-Well, yes. But that's just the kind of world this is, so I'm afraid you'll just have to put up with it…"

The goddess seemed troubled as she said that, but I was going to give her another push.

"Yes, I'm fully aware of that... However, the God of Earth said he would 'ask you to take care of me.' You yourself even talked about how you would give me some 'extra service' earlier."

"Mmgh... T-True, I did say that... Very well then, what else would you like?"

Aw hell *yeah!*

"An Item Box."

"...What?"

"An Item Box."

"And what would this, um, 'Item Box,' be?"

I thought you'd never ask!

"For someone as lacking in strength as myself, it'd be impossible to carry the items, equipment, water, food, and whatever else that may be necessary to travel in this world. Not only that, but if I were to carry all my money and valuables with me all the time, I'd be sure to be attacked by pickpockets or bandits. The same goes for leaving my belongings at an inn; this is a world where I can't even trust the people working at the inn, let alone the other patrons staying there. I just wouldn't feel safe about that. No matter how hard I work, I'd never be able to save any money, which would make moving to another town of my own accord extremely difficult. How exactly would I be able to live a happy life like that?"

"Mngh..." The goddess winced.

"That's where the Item Box comes in! It's a storage device connected to an alternate dimension with infinite capacity, and because time is frozen inside it, anything put inside will never deteriorate. I can take things out or put things in whenever I like, and it's impossible for it to be used by anyone else. If I put my money and other belongings in it, then I don't have to worry about anything being stolen, or having luggage so heavy I wouldn't be able to move anywhere. This power is the bare minimum that is absolutely imperative for my day-to-day life, wouldn't you agree?"

"I-I see… This 'Item Box' seems to be quite the convenient object. Did everyone use one back on the world the other God oversees?"

"Oh no, it was pretty easy to carry luggage around back on Earth, and you wouldn't really have to worry about your stuff because of how safe it was back there. Ahaha…"

I managed to play that off pretty well, I think.

"Then I will begin the final checks: Your body will be the same genetically, and back to how you were at fifteen years old. Earth's supervisor provided your genetic information, so there's no need to worry about that. The people of this world are said to come of age at fifteen years old as well, with the marriageable age for aristocrats between fifteen to eighteen years old, and fifteen to twenty-two for commoners, so I believe that will be a suitable age for you. Oh, and aristocrats are usually quick to make marriage engagements, so them getting married as soon as they come of age is actually quite common. Once you pass eighteen, you're considered 'late to the marriage party,' and going past twenty means you're in trouble. As for the commoners, people from more rural areas usually marry earlier for various reasons, such as to lower the cost of food, for more manpower, or because they want to hurry up and have a child. In the city, however, the average age is generally somewhere between seventeen and twenty-two. Around twenty-three, they start getting really desperate; at twenty-four they're at the end of their rope; and by the time they reach twenty-five and twenty-six, they have this dead look in their eyes."

Well, crap, that's pretty harsh... Gotta do my best getting married!

"Continuing on... As per your request, you will receive the ability to understand, read, and write in any language; the power to create any medicine with the exact effect you imagine it to have, in any container you are thinking of; and finally, an Item Box spell that connects to an interdimensional storage with unlimited space, where time doesn't pass inside of it, which you can access at any time, anywhere, and it cannot be used by anyone else but you. I don't really understand what this Item Box is, but I'll make it so it reflects whatever you imagine it to be, so be sure to keep a clear image of it in your head. Now, is there anything wrong with what I just said?"

Yup, that's all perfect. Now, for the finishing touches...

"No, there's nothing wrong with that. To finish, I have a few questions, and one more request to make. Is that all right?"

"Of course, feel free to ask me anything."

The goddess had a look on her face that showed how relieved she was this would finally be over soon. *All right, guess I'll ask her.*

"The first thing I'd like to ask about is the religious situation in this world. There's nothing scarier than religion, after all. What are they like here?"

"Ah, that's an easy one. Almost all the religions of this world believe I'm the one and only God, and they worship me. How they pronounce and write my name varies slightly depending on the sect and the region, but they're all referring to me. The doctrines and laws of each also differ to a certain extent, but since they all split off from the same thing, there isn't much difference between them fundamentally. They admonish any type of discrimination against a person's race or status, so I would say they're relatively moderate religions. I would assume demons and such would be their enemies, but since they don't actually exist, there aren't any problems there."

Hmm… So there was only one religion, huh. I didn't know if that wasn't a problem, or was a really big one.

"Then would it be bad if someone formed a new religion, or if the current one were to die out?"

"No, I wouldn't really mind. It's not like I'm actually a god, after all. I'm just part of a long-lived and ancient species. Since I end up driving humans away, due to my adjustments to the world and getting rid of distortions, it's more convenient for them to think of me as a divine being, so I don't try to dissuade them. However, I'll also sometimes send out 'divine revelations' to save them from great disasters and the like. My existence and the role I play have nothing to do with faith, but I'm fine with playing the part of a fictional goddess if it means imparting beneficial teachings that support the lives of the people. While there aren't any significant problems regarding the doctrine of the religion, there hasn't been anything to oppose it all this time, and corrupt priests are beginning to spread like wildfire. There wouldn't be any problems if the religion were to disappear, really. After all, it's been fifty years since the last time I sent a revelation to this world, though sometimes you'll find people claiming to be the 'new oracle,' but that's nothing more than an egregious lie.

"…Now I'm starting to get mad. Maybe I'll send down some divine punishment for the first time in a few hundred years…"

Whoa, whoa, whoa, slow down! If you're going to do that, do it later, and somewhere far *away from me!*

"Th-Then on to my next question… Would it be bad to do anything that would influence the world on a large scale? Like, for example, if I were to spread techniques or ways of thinking from back on Earth."

"Hm? No, I wouldn't mind that at all, really. My job is to keep the space-time continuum stable, so I don't really plan on doing anything with this world's civilization. If it seemed like a lot of living creatures were going to die for no reason, though, then I might try to lend them a hand. Sometimes I try helping out a particular organism just to kill time, but I never thought once about trying to influence the culture of this world to go in any specific direction. On that point, the supervisor for your world really is amazing, given how he puts so much love and affection into the work he does for life on Earth…"

If you think that, then you should do it too. That way you could have something in common with God to talk about… Oh, hey, maybe I should just tell her that.

"Then why don't you try putting in some more work as well?"

"Oh, no, you have no idea how much of a pain that is. If you don't have enough affection and patience for living things and leave it only halfway done, it turns into a real mess. I made a little mistake doing just that in the past, so I haven't been trying my hand at it lately…"

"But if the God of my world were to see his junior working hard doing the same work he was, don't you think he'd be happy about that? Since you finally managed to make a connection with him now, you could go ask him for advice when you're in trouble or if you messed up on something. It'd be something in common you could both talk about."

"Th-That's it, that's it! Oh, why didn't I figure that out sooner! I'm such an idiot… I'll start preparing to maintain the world again right away!"

Good, just try your best not to mess anything up, okay? You're not going to mess up on purpose just so you can come back to me for more advice, right? I mean, you are *the person in charge of this world, after all.*

"All right, I've got one last question then. You don't have to answer this if you don't want to, it's just something I'm asking out of curiosity. You and the God in charge of Earth both, um… How do I put it… You both talk like humans, even though I think you're both higher life-forms that far surpass the likes of us humans. Despite that, the feelings you have for God are something on the same level as humans, and that feels really strange to me… I'm sorry if I made you feel bad, you really don't have to answer. I just wanted to ask at least once."

It took some courage to ask that question, and there really wasn't any merit in asking it, but I was just so curious I couldn't help myself. If I didn't, I wouldn't be satisfied with why God treated me the way he did, and I wouldn't truly be able to relax and enjoy my life. This also had something to do with whether or not I would make my final request.

"I see… Well, of course you'd be curious about that. Then I'll explain this as simply as I can. If you don't understand or aren't satisfied with something, please think of it as 'that's just how it is.'"

Looks like she was going to tell me after all. The expression on her face seemed like it had just gotten way more serious too… I was getting a powerful sense of intelligence from her eyes that I didn't feel before.

"It is true we are beings that greatly differ from your species. We have no defined physical body, the appearance of myself and the being in charge of Earth being nothing more than a temporary form to match that of you humans. In addition, our mental processes and the speed at which we think are vastly different than those of your race. Not only are we long-lived, our perception of time differs as well.

For that reason, the being you see before you is the consciousness of only one of the numerous parallel thought processes from my true body. This consciousness, which has been given the role of watching over this world, has had its thought processing slowed down to the bare minimum and its intelligence lowered to the extreme for the purpose of interacting with your species.

"But, to be completely honest, this is all quite enjoyable. If I were to explain it in a way you would understand, it would be a sensation similar to watching an infant crawl around, or watching a small child play some silly game, one where you don't have the slightest clue as to why they find it to be entertaining... Something along those lines.

"I don't know if I got the point across well enough or not... Rather, my other, much more intelligent parallel thought processes are enjoying the emotion I am feeling right now. The sense of respect I feel toward the being in charge of Earth is genuine. I, or rather, the foundation that makes up my real body, have a profound respect for that being's true form, which would most likely be the cause of why I hold such strong feelings for them. My current body and real body are one and the same, after all. Just like myself, the supervisor in charge of Earth is only an extremely small portion of the foundation of that being's consciousness, so they seem like a person worthy of my respect for them... Or something like that. And so, considering the situation that being found themselves in, they approached you in earnest and did what they thought was right for you. To be honest, I think they may be a bit excessive in their approach...but that is very much like that being, which is wonderful in and of itself. That is why I want to respect their intentions as much as possible. Was that clear enough?"

As she finished talking, the intense expression on her face reverted back to the happy-go-lucky feeling she had had before. Did she boost her level of intelligence just for that conversation? I felt like that was probably the case. If she didn't, then the difference from how she talked up till now would be too immense. If that was how she normally was, I would've never gotten my Item Box, let alone the other "services" she would provide me. Or maybe all that *was* the "service" she was talking about?

Well, no matter. All I could do now was give it my all in taking on this girl in front of me!

"Yes, I understand… Well, it's not like I understood everything, actually, but I feel like I have a handle on most of it. So, thank you very much. With that, I've asked everything I wanted to. All I have left is one final request."

Swallowing my spit with a gulp, I asked the question:

"Please, um… Please be my friend!"

The goddess froze up, her mouth hanging open.

It's fine, right?! I don't have a single friend in this world! I only had two in the last one, even!

I went woozy for just a moment, but I planted my feet firmly on the ground and waited it out. *All right, I've gotten the hang of this now!* …But even though I was finally used to it, I'd never get another chance to put that experience to use. Probably.

Well, here I was in one of those "other worlds" I'd heard so much about. It was supposed to be called "Verny" or something.

After Celes came out of her cosmic entity mode, she happily agreed to be my friend and threw her arms around me. It seemed her galaxy brain powers only lasted for when she was explaining everything to me. Once she finished, she just went back to her previous, happy-go-lucky self. She spent a good amount of time rubbing up against me, having me think up new ways of her getting closer to God, and a whole bunch of other things as well. When I was finally freed from our little bonding session, that was when I found myself standing in this new world.

It looked like I was standing about halfway up some sort of small hill, and I could see sparse clumps of trees all around me. There was a town way off in the distance, but it wasn't surrounded by walls or anything. Seemed like it was full of fairly normal-looking buildings as far as I could tell.

I should probably be aiming for the town for now, but, before that, I wanted to check out my new body. I'd be spending a long time with it after all, so I wanted to be thorough about it. Had to make sure to send my complaints to Celes if there was anything wrong with it, and I could ask for extra stuff at the same time! Just call me *Kaoru Almighty.* I doubt Celes was going to give me her powers or anything if I kept complaining about her though.

With that, I began running all sorts of tests on myself, including stretching out, jumping around, patting myself down in a bunch of different places; stuff like that. The results: it seemed like I really was back to the body I had when I was fifteen years old. I couldn't check my face since I didn't have a mirror or anything, but it at least felt right from what I could tell. Still, you didn't have to get every single little detail right, Celes! I wouldn't have minded a bit more strength, or some more endurance, or, you know... A little bust enhancement wouldn't have hurt! I would've been completely fine with that!

Dammit...

Height-wise, I thought there was maybe a one centimeter difference between fifteen-year-old me and me at twenty-two, so it didn't feel like much had changed. I was about 157 centimeters, or a little under five feet two inches for all you people stateside. I was a little bit heavier back then too. Instead of thinking about maintaining my body, I had been more focused on things like club activities. And my appetite. Man, I was so young then… (Super serious.)

What I *really* had a beef with was my chest.

Yeah, back when I was twenty-two I could barely call myself a B-cup… But now, sadly enough, I was a solid A. No, this was a rarity! Only one in twenty people in Japan had the privilege of bearing this status nowadays! Celes was the same too, so I guess that meant we matched now. Maybe that was why she was so happy when I asked her if we could be friends…

Wait, Celes had the ability to change how she looked to whatever she wanted to, didn't she? *Grrr…*

Hold on, just calm down, me. Now wasn't the time to get angry at her…yet. *Deep breaths, deep breaths…*

For the time being, the body check was over. Next up, a powers check. I thought I'd give my most important ability a shot: potion creation. I stuck out my right hand and concentrated.

Give me a health potion that tastes like a sports drink!

I tried imagining the container being one of those small, plastic bottles you saw everywhere for drinks. The next instant, I held a bottle from a famous drink company in my right hand, filled to the brim with the exact contents I'd been thinking of. After twisting off the cap and taking a swig, I found it really did have the slightly bittersweet taste of a sports drink. I wasn't tired or anything, so I wasn't really sure if it was healing me at all, but I was going to put my faith in Celes and believe it must have some sort of effect if I could already do this much.

The next thing I needed to check was my Item Box of course!
Item Box, open!

I concentrated and poured everything I had into focusing my mind as I stuck my right hand out. It wasn't like I really had to do all that, apparently, but since this was my momentous first use of the Item Box, I wanted to make it seem as cool as possible.

As I slipped my wrist inside an invisible space in the air, a list of my inventory appeared inside my head.

[Inventory: Empty]

…Yeah, I knew that was going to happen…

It wasn't like I was hoping for you to put something in there as a little extra service, Celes. No, not at all… Like, seriously, I wasn't disappointed in the slightest. It wasn't like I was hoping for some sort of divine sword that split heaven and earth, or a whooole bunch of useful items for every situation you could think of, to be stuffed in there for me. Nope, not this girl.

Next time I saw Celes, I thought I'd tell her all about a certain arrogant King of Heroes who loved his flashy gold armor, and maybe some stories about a certain blue cat-thing with a huge pocket on its belly for good measure.

Anyway, it looked like that was that for now. I wouldn't know about the language thing until I met some other people first.

All right, time to head to that town. I bet I'll come across some type of road if I just go down this hill.

I took a big stretch, then lightly brushed off my pants before finally setting off. I made sure to have Celes change my outfit to the type of clothes you'd find in this world before she sent me here. I mean, it'd be kind of a problem for me if she just tossed me into this world stark naked, so I made doubly sure to ask her for clothes. I felt like I could've been in danger if I didn't. Seriously, knowing what she was like, I'd had a really bad feeling about it. My danger senses were going into overdrive, I tell you.

After walking for a little while, I noticed a little squirrel-ish creature staring at me from one of the tree branches above me.

"Hey, you up there in the tree. Is this the right way to get to a town with people in it?"

As I gave it a nonchalant smile, the small critter replied: *"Yup, that's right. Just go straight ahead."*

"Oh, thanks a bunch. You really helped me out!"

"Hey, no problem!"

I walked in silence for a bit, eventually coming to a stop and placing both hands on a nearby tree. I then proceeded to bash my head against it repeatedly.

"Understand, read, and write in any language... UNDERSTAND! READ! AND WRITE! IN ANY! LANGUAGE!!!"

Celes...why did you decide to go that *far with my special service power?!*

That little guy from before couldn't write too, could he? I was beginning to get a little freaked out by that, so I was just going to stop thinking now.

The sun had already gotten pretty low in the sky. The town had *looked* close when I was back on the hill, but it still seemed like I had a ways to go. A little while later, I finally found something that resembled a highway leading to town, but it was still pretty far away. I'd heard things looked much closer than they really were when you were somewhere high up, so I guess this was a prime example of that, huh...

41

I always loved reading, so I had a pretty good repertoire of random knowledge. I even chose a science major in college, and I had a deep respect for all the mad scientists out there who sacrificed everything for the sake of their research. I had no intention of doing anything like that myself, though.

I was starting to get pretty thirsty along the way, not to mention tired, so I ended up downing a bunch more potions along the way. They actually helped me feel more energized, and it killed two birds with one stone, since they slaked my thirst too. There was a drug back on Earth that could get rid of all your fatigue as well, wasn't there? What was it called again? I remembered it was a combination of the Greek words for "love" and "labor," so Philopo…

I was getting freaked out again, so I stopped thinking. Again.

This potion doesn't have any weird side effects to it, right?!

Also, if Celes was supposed to drop me close to town, how come she'd put me so far away? It was dangerous to leave things to Celes. I knew she probably didn't mean anything bad by it, but her basis for judgment was a bit…screwy, to say the least. Well, the way she saw things was probably *way* different than a human would, so I guess that's just how it is. That didn't change the fact that it still felt dangerous to leave it all up to her, so I was just going to try to do my best to get through everything on my own. For now, I was just relieved that I'd made sure to specify that I actually wanted clothes. And I was a little miffed that I'd made it this far with no resistance whatsoever. At this rate, it seemed totally possible that cats were going to end up being the villains here or something.

It was a little bit after the sun had set (there appeared to only be one in this world) that I finally made it into town. It was *just* before it got completely dark outside, so I'd say I was cutting it pretty close.

There were no walls surrounding the town, which meant there were no gatekeepers here either. It seemed like people could come and go as they pleased.

It wasn't like it was the royal capital or a huge bustling city or anything. It was just a small rural town that didn't hold any strategic value whatsoever. I'd bet there wasn't really any benefit to using all the money you'd need to build the walls surrounding the town, pay the costs to maintain them, pay the people necessary to staff them, and just deal with the general inconvenience of it all. I'd have been in a bit of a jam if you needed some sort of ID to get in and out of town, so I was thankful for that.

I went ahead and made four healing potions before I headed into town: three blue ones and a single yellow one. I wanted to make more than that, but I was empty-handed at the moment. I didn't even have a bag to carry my stuff in. I might get myself into trouble if I suddenly used my Item Box without knowing what did and didn't fly in this world, and I would look like a total weirdo if I just carried everything in my hands.

I ended up shoving two potions into each of the chest pockets on my clothes. I arranged them by color according to a game I had played a long time ago. There were three types of healing potions: blue, yellow, and red, with each one more potent (and valuable) than the last. Since it was so easy to tell them apart at a glance, I decided to adopt those colors for my own labeling system as well. The blue ones were just your run-of-the-mill potions and could heal your everyday external wounds like gashes and bruises; that sort of thing. Yellow was your intermediate potion, and fixed up things like internal damage and broken bones in addition to the other wounds the blue could. Finally, you had your red potions, which were powerful enough to bring you back from the brink of death, but you'd probably want to wait and see if the situation could be solved by taking a blue or yellow potion first. My policy would be to wait at least a day before deciding to use a red potion.

I'd make my goal for today to get enough money for dinner and a place to sleep, so there was no reason for me to take any risks while I still didn't know up from down in this world.

I headed along the main road until I found an inn, so I could check out their rates. A night at the inn with dinner and breakfast cost four silver coins. I guessed a silver coin was something like 1,000 yen, then? If that was the case, then I guessed my blue potions were worth one coin, and my yellow one about five? Well, I should be fine for tonight, so long as I could scrounge up about five coins.

Following that, I decided to head to the Hunter's Guild right away, after asking a nearby hunter where it was.

Welp, I'd say the building in front of me definitely seemed like the Hunter's Guild.

There was a mark on the front with a sword and a spear clashing with each other, and the sign on the front said "Hunter's Guild." *All right, I can actually read it!* The place had swinging doors that looked like they were right out of a Western flick. I didn't know if it was because it was nighttime or what, but those swinging doors were the only things being kept open, while the normal doors were shut tight. I bet it was the opposite during the day—so long as it wasn't winter, or the weather was bad, or something.

Hrm... It was kinda hard to get myself to go inside... But if I didn't go in there, then I could say goodbye to having dinner and a place to sleep tonight...

I steeled myself and finally made my way through the door. I shouted out, "Anyone here!" in my mind…but in reality, I slipped in through the barely ajar doors without saying a word. Life was cruel, however, and the bell hanging above the door made the loudest jangling sound you could imagine as I snuck inside, causing everyone in the room to stare directly at the entrance to the guild—and at me.

It looked like working hours were over for most of the receptionists here, since most of the counters were completely devoid of people. Only one of them was still open… I wondered if that was the nighttime service counter or something, but no one was lined up there.

In stark contrast with this side, the area just behind the counters was roaring with activity. There were tons of tables all lined up over there, with people who were probably hunters stuffing their faces and downing all kinds of alcohol as they chatted away with each other. It looked like there was some sort of counter way in the back providing food and drinks for everyone. Yeah, these kinds of places always seemed to be set up like this.

Wait, shouldn't this be the part where someone says, "Hey, this ain't no place for a kid," or something? Or maybe, "Hey there, little missy, how's about pouring us another glass of the good stuff?" You know, something like that…

Huh? Were they ignoring me? I mean, it wasn't like I wanted to get involved or anything… It was just, I had my pride as a woman. And I felt like that pride was slowly being chipped away… No, it was nothing! I was just going to head over to that counter now like a good girl!

And so here I was. I'd made it to the nighttime counter.

The receptionist here looked pretty intense, and she gave off a harsh vibe… But I bet she didn't want to hear that from me, especially when people always told me that *I* was the one who always had a harsh look in her eyes. There were no other counters open right now, so it looked like I had to take my chances with the scary lady.

"Um, excuse me…"

She's totally glaring at me! But still, I couldn't back down now. My dinner and my place to stay were both riding on this. All those potions I drank earlier were sloshing around in my stomach right now, but I wanted some actual, solid food, dang it! Oh, and a soft bed as well, of course.

"Erm… Is it possible for me to sell potions here?"

"You're kidding me, right?"

Eep!

"What are potions? Some type of medicine? Go to the apothecary if that's what you have. Why would you even bring them to the Hunter's Guild? Are you stupid or something?"

Shot down…

Right, so this wasn't the right place to sell potions… Then that meant I had to at least try to move on to the next step!

"I'm sorry, this is my first time leaving my hometown in the sticks, so I don't really know anything… If I don't sell these, I won't be able to eat or find a place to stay tonight. Where could I find the apothecary and the doctor?"

"Yeah, fat chance either of them would be open right now. Besides, the doctor is out of town for a while; he's off to a nearby village. The apothecary went to a neighboring town to see a couple that just got married. Seems like they had a kid or something. I'd say they'll probably both be back sometime tomorrow or the next day, though."

Ahhhhhh… It's all over…

I slumped down to the floor, my dreams of hot food and a warm bed fading into nothingness. Why didn't Celes have any money ready for me before she set me loose here?!

…The answer was simple, of course: *because she was Celes.*

Damn it, damn it, damn iiiiiit! My tears were completely blurring my vision at this point.

Thankfully for me, it looked like the sharp-eyed receptionist had a heart of gold after all. After watching my miserable breakdown, she took pity on me and came to my rescue.

"All right, guess there's no way around it… I'm in charge of the place till morning, so I'll use my authority to help you out a little. I'll say it now, but this is only for tonight, got it? There's no 'next time' for this, even for the days I'm on duty again!"

"Y-Yes, I got it! Thank you very much!"

A drowning woman would take any lifeline she could get, and it was safe to say I was pretty desperate right now.

"Then first off, I'll let you borrow one of the folding beds we use for employees who need some emergency shut-eye. I can't actually let you into the staff-only area or anything like that, so you'll have to make do with one of the corners around here. If you come crying to me about how the floorboards are too hard or your blanket is too thin or something, I'm tossing you back out on the streets!"

"U-Understood!"

"Next up is food. I don't plan on giving you any kind of money, so you'll have to do something about that on your own. I'll be nice and give you permission to work here for the night, so go earn your dinner money by selling your potions or whatever to those hunters back there. You could also run errands, rub their shoulders, or pour them drinks or something. That could also be a good way to get them to share some of their food with you... However!" The receptionist slammed a hand on the counter for emphasis. "HOWEVER! No selling your body, got that?! If you do, I'll beat you AND the guy who paid for you half to death before kicking you out, so make sure that sits tight in that pretty little head of yours!"

She glared even harder at me with those piercing eyes of hers. Even though I was able to pull off being pretty firm with God and Celes, I wasn't about to push my luck with the receptionist from hell here. I bowed over and over to express my gratitude before scurrying off to the dining hall packed with tipsy patrons. If the doctor and apothecary were out of town, then I should have plenty of chances to peddle my potions to everyone.

The receptionist's shouts rang throughout the dining hall, clearly audible for everyone to hear. Despite the harsh look in her eyes, the hunters were all totally on board for doing anything they could to help the cute young girl with her plight. Not to mention they were all pretty used to women with harsh expressions thanks to the receptionist, Gilda.

Kaoru looked to be about fifteen years old...but that was only if she were still in Japan. To the people from the land of the rising sun, Westerners who were twelve or thirteen looked like high schoolers, or even college students if they were unlucky enough. The opposite was also true, of course. There were plenty of cases where Westerners would mistake fully grown Japanese women for children. To this day, that they would be given all sorts of candy and treats when traveling abroad never ceased to baffle these women.

In this world, people looked at Kaoru like she was around twelve years old at best—the sharp-eyed receptionist included. If she actually did look to be fifteen or older, there was a chance everyone here wouldn't have been this nice to her. It was possible they could have told her to put up with an empty stomach for a night and just sleep outside since she was an adult. No matter what world you ended up in, it seemed like children and all the beautiful people were still the only ones to get special treatment.

"Would anyone care for a potion? The blue potions can heal any type of cut or wound, and they only cost one silver coin! The yellow one can cure everything from broken bones to internal damage, all for the low price of five silver coins!"

That was the sales pitch Kaoru tried going with, but all she got from the hunters she was trying to help were bitter smiles. A single silver coin could buy about three or four mugs of ale, and all it would take was another silver coin to get you a decent amount of food and other snacks. No matter how much they wanted to help her, they weren't about to cough up a silver coin for medicine a kid probably made out of weeds or something. They might have been able to at least laugh it off and call it some type of diet supplement if she made it cheaper, but that would only be if it was for a few copper coins. They would've sprung for a small silver coin at most.

Kaoru was beginning to panic once she realized the potions she was so proud of probably weren't going to sell.

Why can't I sell these? There seem to be plenty of injured hunters here from what I can see.

Were they planning on having their friends heal them up with magic later? Maybe they had to rely on potions when they were on the job and didn't have a healer in their party, but they could get healed on the cheap from another party's healer when they were back in town. It was true you probably didn't need to worry about MP once you were back, and they may be able to get fixed up for the same price it would cost to treat them to a drink or something...

Crap, I made my prices too high! But, wait... They should need potions for when they're out there on the job too. I could be making all sorts of trouble for myself if I make them too cheap... What should I do?!

A tough, middle-aged hunter called out to Kaoru as she agonized over her next move.

"Hey, little missy, think you could rub my right leg for me? I think I might've been a bit too rough with it today, since it feels like it could cramp up any second. Man, that'd hurt like hell if it did. How about we make your payment these two sausages here?"

"One leg rub, coming right up!"

Kaoru happily bounded over to the man out of sheer joy. She'd always given her mom and dad massages for tips, so she was fairly confident in her skills. The hunter was just about the same age as her dad as well, so she didn't shy away from doing it at all. It was almost the exact same feeling as when she would do it to her dad. Besides, who could say if the man really was feeling like he would cramp up, or if he simply made it up as an excuse to give Kaoru something to eat? No matter the reason, the hunter's eyes were half-closed in pure bliss, as Kaoru put her all into massaging his leg, which was around the time the other hunters saw that and started getting rowdy.

"Do me next! My shoulders need a good rubbin', and I'll give ya two of these chicken skewers for it."

"I've got a quarter of a boar steak for ya if ya can gimme a back massage!"

"All that's gonna get stuck in her throat if you lot just keep giving her food! Here, I've got a mug of grape juice for you! That's *way* more valuable than these scraps they keep trying to give you!"

"Damn... Then, I've got fruit! Go ahead and ask me for anything you want! Oh, but peaches're out of the question. Those things are *way* too expensive!"

"Oh, come on, you lazy bum! It's the hunter's spirit to act tough. Man up, and *get the girl a peach, dammit!*"

"B-But..."

The fierce-looking receptionist took a look back at the dining hall, raising her eyebrows somewhat. It even looked like the corners of her mouth were pulled up ever so slightly. Perhaps you could call that a smile on her part, though there were very few hunters who'd believe that theory. That went *especially* for those who knew just what type of personality she had.

After a short while of Kaoru being fed by the hunters, she finally managed to say, "Please, no more food! I'm stuffed, so I'll take copper coins if you can spare them!" which the hunters gladly obliged.

Suddenly, the doors to the guild were flung wide open. It happened a little while after Kaoru had eaten her fill and was starting to get paid in copper coins.

A female hunter who looked to be in her mid-twenties came bursting into the guild, shouting, "Someone show me where a doctor is, I've got someone seriously wounded here! Tell them to get their clinic open!"

Just a second later, a man around his early thirties with a well-defined physique rushed in carrying another blood-soaked man on his back. They were followed by an archer who looked like he had just turned twenty, who was carrying a sword and some armor, which probably belonged to the injured man.

"He got done in by a graybear!" the man shouted as he carried his wounded comrade, "Please, we have to hurry!"

The receptionist came running out from behind the counter, her usual intimidating demeanor replaced by a more serious expression. Facing the four who just came in, she told them the one thing they didn't want to hear:

"Doctor's gone to one of the nearby settlements and won't return for some time. The apothecary's also left for a neighboring town. I dunno if they'll return by tomorrow, or sometime later than that. All the hunters here are familiar with emergency first-aid techniques, so our only hope is to cooperate with 'em, while using any medicinal herbs you may have on hand…"

Expressions of despair clouded the party members' faces. Anyone here could tell these weren't the type of wounds that could be handled by amateurs. They laid the injured man down on a blanket spread out on one of the tables, standing around in a daze.

"What are you all doing?!" Kaoru shouted, "We need to hurry up and cast a healing spell on him! With this many hunters, there should be at least one or two healers around, right?! Also, you should be giving them your high-grade potions, a person's life is on the line here! You can just get them to pay you back afterward! Why are you all just standing around?! C'mon, guys!"

The hunters continued standing where they were, blank expressions on their faces, as if they couldn't comprehend what Kaoru was yelling about in her sudden outburst.

"Forget it, just get out of the way! I'll do it!"

She pushed aside the people standing in her path to make it to the table where the injured man lay. His armor was already off, so she went ahead and swiped a knife from the middle-aged man who carried him in to begin cutting away the parts of his clothes near his injuries. His wounds were now out in the open, blood still pouring from the gashes.

"H-Hey…"

Kaoru ignored the flustered man. She didn't have time to deal with him now.

"Somebody bring me the strongest alcohol you've got, bottle and all! Hurry!"

With dumbfounded responses, a few of the hunters ran off to the food and drink counter and brought back many bottles of booze with them. Kaoru used her teeth to pull out the corks before dousing the man's wounds with the contents of the bottles. The injured man had been unconscious up till now, but as soon as the alcohol touched him, his back arched and he screamed bloody murder.

"I know it hurts, but it beats being dead! Pain is proof you're still alive!"

The men didn't say a word. They could only stand around watching, their eyes wide as Kaoru took one of the potions she had made from her pocket—the yellow one, specifically. She held it out toward the female hunter who had come rushing into the guild first.

"Make him drink this! I only have one of the yellow kind, so don't spill it!"

Maybe it was because the woman got the hint from the intensity of Kaoru's expression, or maybe it was because she just wanted some hope to cling to, but she silently nodded and took the yellow potion. She moved the injured man's head so his neck was completely straight, then took some of the potion inside her own mouth. She grabbed the man's chin to open his mouth, then used mouth-to-mouth to feed him some of the potion.

She did it twice, then a third time, until the entirety of the yellow potion had made it down the injured man's throat. At the same time, Kaoru was pouring the blue potion directly onto the man's wounds. Not only was the alcohol she asked for earlier acting as a disinfectant, but she was using it to wash away the blood and dirt, as well, so she could apply her potions directly onto his injuries.

She took out a second blue potion and drenched him in it as well. That's when the effects began appearing, and dramatically at that.

The flame of life had looked to be all but extinguished from the man when he first came in, but, after he drank the yellow potion and had two blue potions poured on his injuries, the deathly pallor in the man's face was replaced with color once more. Not only that, his once-torn skin bubbled and swelled as it knitted itself back together again before everyone's eyes. He'd already stopped bleeding, and his breathing had become stable. His injuries alone hadn't been enough to bring him to death's door in a single blow, but rather, he'd been brought to the brink of death due to a significant amount of time passing after suffering so much internal damage and blood loss. That was the reason his wounds didn't call for a red potion, but could be dealt with using a yellow one. Pouring the blue potions directly onto his injuries had proved effective as well. It wasn't a perfect recovery, however, since it wasn't as if the potions could also replace all the blood he'd lost...

But everyone who saw what had just happened knew what it meant: he was going to be all right.

Now that the specter of death no longer loomed over the injured man, the female hunter was clinging to him, while the middle-aged man who carried him in could only stand there in a daze. The young archer, who was carrying all the equipment, had already dropped to the floor.

Maybe it was because he'd been too busy worrying about his injured friend, but the middle-aged man had a deep gash on his left arm that was still bleeding. Kaoru was amazed at just how tenacious and focused he was to carry another man while looking like that. However, he was losing a bit too much blood from his wound. Judging by how deep that gash ran, it would take a considerable amount of time for it to heal, and there was always the chance it could end up leaving a scar. That would be a bit of a waste—no, it would be a *huge* waste for a guy like him. Smoldering middle-aged men were the treasures of all humanity.

Kaoru silently offered her last blue potion to the man.

"Wh-What are you doing?! You think I could just use something as valuable as that on just a few scratches?!"

"Quiet, you. Just shut up and drink!"

"…Y-Yeah, okay…"

After being glared at by Kaoru's trademark harsh eyes, the man obediently took the potion and drank it all down. The next moment, the deep gashes on his arm healed and closed themselves.

The guild hall had fallen into a dead silence, when somebody muttered under their breath: "It's a miracle…"

The next moment, the hall erupted into cheers.

"YEEEAAAHAAAHHH!!!"

"Attagirl, little missy! Attagirrrl!"

"I had her rub my leg! What the hell was I thinking…?!"

"That was to help her out when she was hungry, so there shouldn't be any problems there!"

"Why was I such an idiot?! Why didn't I buy that medicine for a silver coin back then?!"

Mugs were shattered in hearty toasts. The tipsy hunters kept on shouting while Kaoru was being tossed about like a ship in a storm in the middle of it all. It was pandemonium, a scene right out of hell, that was centered around an angel—one that just happened to have a very harsh look in her eyes.

Chapter 3:
The Great Escape

I was totally thrown for a loop. This was all wrong, no matter how you looked at it. This wasn't what Celes and I had talked about at *all*. It was around that time that I came to a realization:

"Ohhh, I get it. Celes totally has a few screws loose."

It was an immediate answer on my part. I didn't need any other information, and there was no need for me to think over it again. Why was I able to come to that conclusion so fast, you ask? Well, luckily for you, I had the perfect reason that should be enough to convince absolutely anyone: *because she's Celes.*

Perfect reasoning, no? It was airtight; no room for any doubts here.

I'd thought something was off about all this... No one used healing magic when there was someone gravely injured in front of them, no one else was selling healing potions here, and everyone was freaking out over the low- and mid-tier potions I'd used.

Celes had said it herself: "Magic, monsters, and hunters exist." In my head, I took "hunters" to mean "adventurers." To be fair, I wasn't that far off the mark there. There were beasts in this world ferocious enough to be called monsters, that was for sure. The "magic" part was where my problem lay.

Magic did exist in this world. Celes said it existed, so it must have. However, that was different than the "mages and priests firing off combat and support spells" or "enchanted magic items and healing potions bonanza" image that I had in my head. The hunters and the Hunter's Guild handled everything from resource gathering to hunting quests and even escort missions. They pretty much took care of everything the adventurers and Adventurer's Guilds you'd hear about in stories back on Earth would. But—and this was a *huge* but (stop laughing)—there was no magic here. *I repeat: THERE'S NO MAGIC HERE!!!*

The only battles were physical encounters with swords, spears, bows, axes, and all that other good stuff. There was nothing different about the weapons here from how they were back on Earth.

Magic, on the other hand, was said to have been created by an eccentric old geezer in a tower somewhere who had devoted his whole life to researching it. He was finally able to use it when he had become senile and was knocking on death's door. These consisted of spells like "squirting one milliliter of water from your hand" and "conjuring a flame about the size of a lit candle wick from the tip of your finger." Friggin' *magic tricks* were more impressive than that! There was no way in hell you could use *that* as your example to say magic existed here!

Huff...huff...huff...

It looked like there was no magic that could actually be put to any sort of practical use in this world. Like the fire breath that dragons could spew out, for example. Or that dragons weren't aerodynamic enough to fly on their wings alone, but they still had the power of flight. Or how dragons had such high defensive abilities, which scales alone shouldn't be able to give them.

Why is it all dragons?! What the hell!

...Anyway, in the midst of all the celebration and revelry, I managed to squeeze some information out of the hunters here. Medical treatment in this world consisted of medicine and salves made from herbs, splints and braces for broken bones, and needle and thread to sew shut any gaping wounds. Magical potions weren't among those options, of course. So here was my conclusion:

...I really screwed myself over, didn't I?

Here were all these fantastic miracle medicines that shouldn't even exist in this world, and the only one who could make them? A helpless little girl with nobody to support her.

I think I may have backed myself into a corner on this one...

Welp, it was time to run away, I'd say.

The next morning, in the main hall of the Hunter's Guild...

On one side you had the receptionist counters, the dining hall on the other, and a kitchen further in the back. Upstairs was where all the business-related rooms were at, which was probably where the big wigs of the place had their offices.

So here I was, in the main hall on the first floor. It was utter chaos, since the mess from the hubbub yesterday still hadn't been cleaned up. There were people waking up with massive headaches, people laid out flat across tables, and even people still out cold and sleeping on the ground. I'd slept on a bunk near one of the walls, but I had to make sure to get up early to get it all put away before things got busy. All I was cleaning up was my bed. A mess in the dining hall? Nope, didn't ring a bell.

I had always been the type of person who had a strict habit of showing up anywhere at least five minutes before I was supposed to be there, which is why I asked Celes to get me a wristwatch. And not some fancy brand name watch that looked like it would break if it smacked into a pole a little too hard, but an actual, functional, tough watch. This thing could withstand water pressure up to one hundred meters deep. If I dove any further than that, I think I would break before the watch did. It was solar-powered, which meant I didn't have to worry about the batteries dying or anything. Actually, I might not need to worry about the battery at all. This thing was made by our favorite goddess after all. The time it displayed was synced with the rotation of this world, and of course I made sure it had an alarm as well. There was no oversleeping for this girl thanks to that.

I wasn't getting plastered like everyone else last night, so I had plenty of time to think things over after I finished my intelligence-gathering mission. My conclusion: I needed to get the hell out of here!

My plan was to get up first thing in the morning and clean up my bed, say thank you to the scary receptionist, then pretend to wander about town before making my escape... But, unfortunately, things weren't going to be that easy for me. It looked like someone had painted a big target on me after what happened last night. Just as I was finished taking care of my bed, I ended up getting caught at the same time.

"So *you* must be Kaoru, girly!"

I was too late...

There were five men in total who had come for me, all working under the orders of some baron dude. The apparent leader of the group looked to be at least somewhat capable, but the other four looked like random thugs from off the streets with leather armor and swords. It looked like they were the "group of thugs that call themselves guards who are working for an influential person" you heard about so much in these types of stories. It seemed they'd managed to grab hold of some people last night who weren't completely smashed and asked them all about this town. Information was money, which meant information was life…or something like that.

Anyway, there was a baron who acted as the governor of this town and a few other villages, and he was trying to get together the money he needed to move up in the world by levying heavy taxes on his territories. Your real stereotypical small-time aristocrat type. Naturally, it seemed like the people hated his guts for that, but I couldn't really imagine a stereotypical aristocrat that was actually loved by the commoners they ruled over.

Excluding the title of "Knight," which couldn't be passed down to your children, barons were at the lowest rank in the aristocracy. They were pretty much the lowest rung of the nobility ladder. Now, if I remember right…the guy had a wife, two sons, and a daughter. I guessed that, after he heard about the incident last night, he must've seen this as his chance to make a fortune and move up in the aristocratic world. I bet he was jumping for joy when he told his lackeys to come after me… But sending five thugs to deal with one little girl was totally overkill. I guess you could say that was to make sure I wouldn't be able to get away, and just in case any of the hunters got in their way.

"Can I help you? My mother always told me never to talk with strangers, and *especially* not to go places with them…"

"What the…" The man who looked to be the leader of the group practically had his eyes popping out of their sockets. "The governor's calling you, so be a good girl and come with us!"

"But I don't live here, you know. I'd follow the orders of the governor where *I'm* from, but why do I have to obey some person who has nothing to do with me? This governor or whoever doesn't mean a thing to me. In fact, they're a total stranger—a stranger who's trying to force a girl to come to their house. And they're not even going through the trouble of doing it themselves either... They're just making their underlings do it for them."

It looked like my comment had the blood rushing to the man's head.

"Y-You little brat!"

By the time he noticed, the hunters were beginning to gather around us.

"Tch, just hurry up and come with us!"

"Ahh!"

The group of men grabbed my arm and forcefully dragged me outside. Even if the hunters wanted to stop these guys, they were all *technically* soldiers working directly under the governor. If things went south, not only could the people who tried to help me end up killed, but their families could be targeted as well. They could only stand there and grind their teeth as they watched us go.

Right then, it looked like I couldn't exactly make a run for it at the moment... At least it didn't seem like I had to worry about them trying to kill me or do other horrible things to me—for now. Then, until I could find that window of escape, I thought it was time to start messing with these guys...

The corners of my mouth curled up into a smile as I thought that.

"Ah, wait, Mr. Soldier! Please don't touch that!"

I made that request to the leader of the group as he kept his grip on my left arm. I was being surrounded on all sides by the other four men after I obediently began walking along with them, which was also the reason why the leader didn't have such a tight grasp on me.

"What, this? Actually, what *is* this…"

The leader looked at me curiously.

I showed off my watch. "It's very expensive, and worth *at least* ten gold coins."

"What?! *Ten* gold coins?!"

To him, this must've looked like a rare accessory the likes of which he'd never seen before.

A large sneer crossed the man's face. "I'll just go ahead and hold onto it, if it's so important."

He snatched the watch from me as I tried resisting him before shoving it into his breast pocket.

Heheh, I totally just made bank on that one! I have to split it with these guys since they saw it, but still…

The leader of the group just couldn't stop smiling.

Of course, I couldn't stop grinning on the inside, either.

The group ended up bringing me all the way to the governor's estate. Even if the baron was on the bottom of the aristocracy's totem pole, he was still nobility, and the most powerful individual in this small domain. Maybe he was just compensating for something, but I had to admit he had quite impressive digs.

Nobody asked who I was as they brought me inside, and I ended up being led to some sort of parlor room. I was passed off to one of the servants waiting outside, and the group of thugs took their leave.

"I have brought Miss Kaoru with me."

After making that announcement to the room, the servant ushered me inside.

Sitting at the table inside, I saw a portly man who I assumed to be the baron himself, a woman who was probably his wife, and three others who I'd have bet were their children: a guy who looked to be around twenty; a boy who was probably about sixteen; and a girl who seemed somewhere between thirteen and fourteen years old. Everyone seemed like they were a bit on the plump side (probably due to a lifestyle of no exercise and rich food). And I didn't know if it was hereditary or something they'd acquired later, but the whole family had this sort of... malicious look in their eyes.

...I should stop judging them based on their eyes. It was making me sad for some reason. Right, it was time to switch to a different train of thought. Yeah.

Okay, so Rodolph is the eldest son, and the daughter and next oldest son are... Agh, I forgot!

Man, I *really* wasn't good when it came to remembering foreign names.

One thing I remembered the hunters telling me about the eldest son Rodolph was his horrible reputation. Apparently, there were plenty of incidents where he acted like he'd already inherited his father's baronial title. I thought that might come in handy later, so I made sure to keep that in mind when I heard it.

The second son was supposed to be pretty decent compared to his older brother, and smart, too. I tried asking around about the daughter, but I didn't manage to wrangle any decent info. An aristocrat's daughter wouldn't really just wander about town, so I guess it made sense there wouldn't be as many rumors about her when compared to the sons.

"Glad to have you here, my dear Kaoru."

The baron gave me a nice broad smile. It was pretty gross having him grin at me like that. Still, this was probably a huge service for me. I mean, not only did someone from the nobility come to greet me with his entire family, he was also being welcoming about it. Not to mention, this particular baron didn't seem to give a rat's ass about the common folk. I was willing to bet something like this wasn't exactly an everyday occurrence here.

"My humblest gratitude for your invitation, Baron." I gave a small curtsey, something I'd learned from watching movies.

"Oho, now would you have a look at that..." The elated baron wore a smile that stretched across his entire face. "Please, have a seat. Allow me to welcome you on behalf of my household."

Baron Renie was absolutely over the moon. He'd been very displeased at first when one of the hunters who worked under him came at an ungodly hour late last night, but was utterly floored after hearing what they had to say: there existed some sort of magical medicine that could heal wounds in an instant. Not only that, but the one who brought it was a little girl with *no one around to protect her*. It was hard for him to believe, but, if it were true, then he could be making more money than he knew what to do with! No, not just something as small-minded as that—becoming an earl, nay, a marquis, may not just be a dream anymore!

This enigmatic medicine was said to be able to bring a person back from the jaws of death in the blink of an eye. Not only was this something he desired for himself, but *all* the nobility would want some of this miracle medicine. Who knew when they would need it for friends and family who might be injured in battle or other unforeseen accidents? He could scarcely even imagine how much money they would pay for it, or what sort of conditions they would accept just to have it... He might even be able to get the royal family in his debt! The baron couldn't believe what good luck he had for this girl to have appeared within his domain. Fortune certainly seemed like it was smiling upon him...

And so, he turned his attention to the girl who had been brought before him. She had well-defined features, and an absolutely dastardly look in her eyes. She reminded him of one of his cousins who used to bully him when he was a child... He showed no fear, however, and feigned being a gracious, aristocratic host as he sat in his chair.

He heard there'd been four vials of this medicine in total. Not just one, but a whopping *four*. Not only that, but she'd tried selling them, and at an absurdly low price. That meant there was more of this medicine somewhere, and she was able to get it *very* easily. If he could get a hold of the person who made it, then he could have a monopoly on production of this miracle cure-all!

Forcing her to spill everything she knew was definitely an option, but there was a chance this girl might not have enough information to go off of. It would be a problem for him if she went and died too easily. There was also the possibility that one of the girl's relatives was making this medicine, and he'd be in trouble if they flat-out refused to listen to him. His best bet here would be to act as friendly as possible to try to appease her. She may have been a petty commoner girl, but he'd made sure to urge his family to feign being as kind as possible to her. Everything should go off without a hitch.

Kaoru felt like she had a rough idea of what the baron was thinking, judging by his suspiciously pleasant attitude. To her credit, she was mostly right.

He introduced her to his family, then they spent some time enjoying tea and expensive snacks while making idle chit-chat. Eventually, while taking great care not to be too impatient, the baron got to the matter at hand.

"By the way, Kaoru, about that medicine you had... Well, just how *did* you get a hold of it? Was there someone who made it that you got it from, perhaps?"

There it was, the *real* reason she was here.

And so, Kaoru gave her answer: "Oh, I made that myself."

"WHAAAAAAT?!"

It wasn't just the baron who had yelled in surprise, but his entire family as well.

"B-By yourself... Does that mean..."

"Correct. I lived together with my father, who worked as an apothecary up in the mountains, where resources were abundant and plentiful. We made and researched medicine together all the time. After he passed away, I tried making my way back to town, but since I've been living in the mountains since I was five, I couldn't seem to figure it out at all..."

The baron thought he was going to fall over, he was so pleased. *She* was the one who made the medicine! This little girl, who had no one around to support her! All with a method that hadn't been made available to the public as of yet!

"Th-Then, do you suppose...you could make it here?" The baron's voice trembled ever so slightly as he asked.

Kaoru, however, flatly gave her response: "That'd be impossible."

"Wh-Why?!"

"It's because someone stole the device I need to make the medicine," Kaoru calmly answered the screaming baron.

"Wh-When was this, and who?!"

"Just a little while ago, and the man who brought me here."

"Call Riche here, NOW!!!" the baron thundered.

Alrighty, if I'm gonna mess up security around here, then I think I'll stir things up a little bit more... Kaoru silently thought to herself.

The man called Riche—the leader of the thugs who'd brought Kaoru here—was brought to the room in response to the baron's summons.

"What can I do for you, Bar—"

"Silence! Return what you stole from this young girl *immediately*!"

His jackpot find was about to be taken away. The man glared at the little girl who had run her mouth too much, but there wasn't anything he could do about it now. Riche reluctantly took what he stole from her earlier from his chest pocket and handed it to the baron.

"There! How about it, is this it?!"

Kaoru took the wristwatch from the baron, inspecting it carefully before she opened her mouth again.

"Ahh… While this is certainly my device, it appears to be broken."

"Wh… Wha…"

Though a nice shade of red just moments earlier, the baron's face had suddenly gone pale. Riche didn't know what was going on, and just stared blankly, stupefied. After all, the accessory in question wasn't broken; he hadn't taken any parts from it, either. That's when Kaoru threw down another bombshell.

"There are plenty of people in the world who wouldn't want you to have my medicine. Not only did he steal it from me, he even made sure to break it as well. What kind of *horrible* person wouldn't want you to recover in case you were injured? I wonder if there are any people out there who would even benefit from something like that…"

Kaoru casually sent a glance toward Rodolph as she threw that out there. Meeting her gaze, he stared blankly back at her, before the color drained from his face once he realized the meaning behind her words.

"Wh-what are you…?" the baron let out.

By the time the baron looked over at Rodolph, his once dazed expression was already long gone, along with all the color in his face. The only thing to see was the baron's eldest son, looking like he'd completely lost his composure. It was almost as if the reason Rodolph seemed so nervous…was because Kaoru's words had found their mark.

Who was the one who would inherit the title of baron if the current baron died? *Rodolph.* Who might feel like he was in danger of losing that title to the baron's more competent second-oldest son? *Rodolph.* Who had invited the baron to go on a hunting trip this week for the first time in what seemed like forever? *Rodolph.*

An oppressive silence had settled over the room. Though Kaoru was the mastermind behind this little chain of events, she couldn't help but squirm over how much she didn't want to be here anymore.

"Sorry, but can I leave now?"

That wasn't going to happen, of course, and Kaoru was instead led to one of the guest rooms. Before that though, she didn't forget to ask the baron if it was all right to have a maid bring her the parts she would need to fix her 'device.'

I was left all alone in the guest room. I covered the doorknob with a cloth so they couldn't peek through the keyhole. I went ahead and opened the curtains as well. We were on the second floor, after all, and it'd be harder for anyone to get close to the window if I had it wide open like this. Didn't want anyone trying to spy on me through the cracks in the curtain either.

I had asked the maid to bring me things like scissors, a file, and a whole bunch of other tools as well. Had to make it seem like I was actually trying to "fix" something, and I was thinking about just hocking everything once I busted out of here. I was flat broke, dang it! I made sure to order a bunch of food as well: sausages, candy, and all that other good stuff. Though the maid warned me it was almost lunchtime, I told her I didn't want to look like a pig stuffing my face when I was in front of the baron, which convinced her to bring me what I asked for. The real reason, of course, was so I could stuff all of it into my Item Box for later. I was slowly getting everything ready to break myself out of here.

Oh yeah, and I had my potion-making abilities handy to take care of drinks, so there were no problems there.

By the time lunch came around, things seemed to have settled down from earlier. I guessed that, once they calmed down and thought it over, nobody would think the baron's barely twenty-year-old son would do anything like that. It seemed like he was let off the hook without anyone really grilling him about it. *Darn.*

On the other hand though, I didn't see that Riche guy around anywhere.

I wonder if me pulling a Maya and passing along all those messages through the maid worked... Like, "It hurt having my arm twisted," and "I'm scared he's going to get violent or try to take away what's precious to me again," or my favorite, "I shake so much when I see him that I can't repair my device." Well, I guessed it was true he could just be out and about, or off somewhere else. Oh, and "pulling a Maya" just meant putting on a performance that rivaled the main girl from this famous shoujo manga (it was about acting, from way back in the day), especially so you could trick or deceive someone. It was a classic.

Conversation at the table was sparse. There wasn't much common ground for aristocrats to talk about, and that went even doubly for me, the girl who was born and raised in another freakin' world. The baron had asked me how the repairs were coming along, and I made sure to tell him it would take a few days. It'd be just peachy if that made him think I wouldn't try running away so long as I was absorbed in fixing my thingie. But still, nighttime was a long way away. They brought me here first thing in the morning, after all!

Finally, I made it to dinner. After safely wrapping up our mealtime conversation without incident, I went ahead and made another request to the baron.

"Would it be all right to have another girl who's just about on the same wavelength as me to help me out?"

"And what would you mean by 'wavelength'?"

"Oh, it just means someone who's compatible with the waves that magical energy gives off."

I made up some random crap to explain it, and the baron allowed it without a second thought. Why wouldn't he? There were no downsides to it for him, since not only would this girl keep a lookout over me, he could also have her report on how the repairs were coming along.

After carefully scrutinizing my options, I decided to go with a young maid who was probably about fifteen or sixteen years old, with blonde hair down to her shoulders and a pair of emerald green eyes. I told her that she could chill in her room for now, and that I wanted her to come by later when I called for her.

With that, I headed back to the guest room they had given me.

The evening wore on, and, soon enough, everyone was fast asleep except for the staff working the night shift. I slowly opened the door to my room to find a guard standing right outside. It was supposed to seem like he was there to protect me, but I already knew he was supposed to keep me from running away.

"Call that girl for me, please."

With a nod, the soldier retrieved the maid who was waiting on standby in a nearby room.

I spent a good while having her do things like place her hand on the watch and concentrate *really* hard on it, and all sorts of other pointless stuff, as I waited for my chance. When that time came, I declared that I was hungry and asked the maid if she could get some tea and snacks. The girl immediately left, then came back just barely ten minutes later with a light meal, a pot of tea, and a bunch of dishes all stacked onto a trolley. *Dang, that was fast...* I wondered if they already had a late-night snack prepared for me because rumors of my supposed "huge appetite" had spread or something.

The girl closed the door and began pushing the trolley into the room. Right when she was close enough to me, I grabbed her hand to pull her away from the cart and got her closer to the bed. While she was totally unaware of what was going on and at my mercy, that was when I pressed the handkerchief against her face.

With the maid now laying down in bed, I was busy stuffing anything and everything I could from the room into my Item Box. First up was the dresser. There were a few dresses in there that I could only assume used to belong to the baron's daughter once upon a time, but I wondered if he put those there for me or something. If anything, I could at least say it seemed his daughter wasn't as chubby back when she wore these.

Next on the list were the candlesticks, the pictures on the wall, the desk, the chairs, the carpet, the spare change of sheets in the chest of drawers, then, upon further consideration, the chest of drawers. Everything on the trolley was going in as well, of course, but I wasn't taking the trolley itself with me; not yet. The real reason I asked for all these snacks wasn't just to build up a stockpile of food, but because I had a feeling I could hock the type of tableware aristocrats used for a tidy profit. And there was one more reason as well...

When I was just about finished packing away my loot, I stripped the girl and changed into her outfit while I packed away my own clothes. I made sure to save her at least one of the spare bedsheets and covered her with it. After I got her down off the bed, I packed it away too. I spread out a towel on the floor, then used the scissors the maid had brought me to snip off my hair so it came just down to my shoulders, the same length as the girl out cold on the floor. I balled up the towel—my freshly cut hair and all—and tossed that in my Item Box as well, then placed the white, frilly maid headdress I took from the girl on my head.

And for the cherry on top: a potion. The one I just downed would change the hair color and eyes of whoever drank it. After I finished that off, I placed my hands on the cart.

The door slowly opened, and a girl exited the room. After making a curtsy while facing the door, the blonde-haired maid stayed slightly bent over her trolley as she deliberately made her way toward the kitchen. The guard posted outside had no interest in children, so he barely even glanced at her. His mind was occupied thinking about the curvy maid who was just hired the other day, trying to find ways to keep himself occupied and get through the long, long hours until morning came...

There wasn't a soul to be seen this late into the evening. Kaoru packed the trolley away into her Item Box and snuck away from the baron's residence. Even if anyone were to see her now, they would most likely think she was just a maid running errands for a guest, or, at most, maybe she was off to have a little rendezvous with a boy or something. They probably wouldn't even take a second glance at her as they pretended not to see her.

In the end, Kaoru's breakout was a success, and she made her escape without her being spotted by anyone. With that, she disappeared into the night.

The following were Kaoru's conditions for picking the girl who would "help her":

They had to have hair and eye colors completely different from her own. Moreover, their hair had to be much shorter than hers, and at a length where the difference was night and day. Finally, they needed to be around the same height and body type as her. The girl unfortunate enough to meet those criteria was sleeping in a room where even the carpet had been whisked away. The handkerchief that had been pressed against the girl's face had been soaked in a potion which, if you breathed in even the slightest amount, would knock you out, but would leave no negative side effects.

The girl Kaoru had thought to be fifteen or sixteen…was actually only twelve years old.

The next morning…

The baron's estate was in an uproar. When a maid had arrived at the guest room to announce that breakfast was served, all she found was a room devoid of furniture, decorations, and carpet. The only thing there was a young maid wrapped in bedsheets. There wasn't even a trace left of the girl the baron was so keen about.

The strength drained from the maid who discovered the barren room, and she fell to the floor on the spot. After sending the guard who saw everything flying, the baron immediately sent out a search party to capture Kaoru. He found himself with a severe lack of people at his disposal, however, and he'd chased away Riche in a fit of anger yesterday, the one person he could count on the most for something like this. Out of options, the baron unwillingly made his way to the Hunter's Guild himself.

"...You'd like us to not only search for a girl, but take her into custody?"

"That's right! I'll pay you handsomely, so hurry and get people together to do so at once!"

The receptionist gave a curt response in the face of the baron's hysterics.

"As I'm sure you are already aware, all fees for requests must be paid up front. The Hunter's Guild doesn't afford anyone special treatment, no matter if they're nobility or a baron. Also, I must mention that we don't accept quests where only the one who finds the target is paid. Please make sure to prepare payment for each person you'd like to take on your request. Keep in mind that the search period will be determined by the amount you pay, and please be sure to have a separate reward for when the job's completed."

"Yes, yes, now hurry up and send people out already!"

"That will happen *after* you provide the fee."

"Damn it! I'll be right back, so just you wait!"

The baron frantically rushed back to his mansion to procure the money he needed for the request. The main hall fell deathly silent, until the receptionist's voice cut through it loud and clear:

"Hey, looks like our lil' angel made her escape!"

"Gyahahahahaha!"

Her words were met with an explosive torrent of laughter.

"Like hell anyone'd take *that* job!" someone yelled out.

"Tch, tch, tch," the receptionist rebuked him, "That's what makes you such an idiot. Of course we're going to take it—*all* of us. But first, we need to make sure we're nicely compensated by our baron friend. Next, we're going to have sightings of her coming in from all over the place, like, 'We saw her in the forest but she got away,' or, 'We found a scrap of her clothing on a cliff' or something. And if we ever happen to run into the baron's search party, we'll have to make sure we tell them the good news, won't we? There may be times our eyes play tricks on us, or we just happen to get a wrong report, but there's nothing to be done about that, right?"

"That's our receptionist from hell for ya! You're cold-blooded, Gilda!"

A folder of papers found their mark and smacked the man foolish enough to say that, and the raucous sounds of laughter continued ringing out from inside the Guild.

Around that same time, Kaoru had succeeded in making her escape from the baron's mansion and the town, and was still in the middle of her getaway. Since she'd been walking all through the night, she was already long gone from the tiny area under the baron's control. Things could get hairy if the baron decided to send his private army into territories owned by other aristocrats, and she would undoubtedly be captured and spirited away again. She still had to be on the lookout for potential pursuers.

She'd already made sure to use another potion to dye her hair silver, since she wanted it to be different than her original hair color, and definitely not the blonde from when she had finally broken free from the baron's mansion. She'd also long since changed out of the maid outfit and into one of the dresses she took from the chest of drawers. She picked the most plain-looking one she could find and tore off all the frilly extras to make it seem more like something a commoner would wear.

There was enough food stored up to last a good few meals, and she had nothing to worry about for hydration, either. All that was left now was to make it to her next goal without being jumped by bandits, and everything would be golden. She'd have nothing to complain about if she could replenish her stockpile of food and acquire herself a new mode of transportation, but life just wasn't going to be that easy. There wouldn't be anything to worry about if she could pack her Item Box full of food at least once, but she hadn't had the chance to do so even once since arriving here.

Looking behind her, she could see clouds of dust far off in the distance, as well as what looked like horses galloping in her direction. Just to be safe, she went off the beaten path to take a breather while hiding behind some trees. Everyone needed a break once in a while, after all. It wasn't like she was in a huge rush to get anywhere, either. As long as she kept checking behind herself on a regular basis, it'd be much easier for her to spot the people on horseback coming than it would be for them to spot a girl traveling on foot. No problems there.

Kaoru had been reborn in the Kingdom of Brancott and was currently aiming for the country's royal capital: Aras. Its population was massive, and since it was a place that attracted all sorts of people, it was the perfect spot for someone to blend in and disappear.

There were tons of nobility living there, but that actually acted as a good deterrent to make sure any particular member of the aristocracy couldn't do whatever they pleased. On top of that, it was a great place for her to gather information. The capital should be chock full of all sorts of helpful wisdom for her to pick up on, and she was thinking it might be a good place for her to finally settle down. That it had a library was another big draw for her.

She had no plans to travel to any other countries at the moment. She barely knew anything about the country she was in right now after all, and it was just too much of a risk to head anywhere else without looking into what kind of international affairs were going on in this world.

It was around evening when she arrived at the next town. She wasn't going anywhere near it of course, as there was too much of a risk that the baron might have already sent his subordinates there ahead of her. So, stepping off the main road, she took a wide detour to go around it. Even though this was the first town she'd made it to since making her great escape, they wouldn't be dumb enough to not lay some sort of trap to try to catch her. Her hair and eyes may be a different color, but Kaoru would be SOL if there was someone who recognized her face.

She would have to put off shopping and selling off her plunder for another time. For now, she would spend the night camping out far away from town. Remembering to make a beast-repelling potion for herself was just the icing on top.

Another three days passed. After taking care to avoid a good number of villages and other settlements, Kaoru had arrived at a decent-sized town.

It had already been four days since she had made her escape, and the baron had probably given up on finding her after this much time had passed. Trying to capture a little girl, who wasn't even one of his citizens, outside his own territory…it would only make him a criminal. It didn't matter that he was a baron; the iron hammer of the law would probably be brought down on him if he tried pulling anything now. There were no privileges he could invoke or claims he could make to get at Kaoru any longer. If anyone tried coming after her, all she had to do was make as big a commotion as possible to get the people around her to step in and help.

I think I should be good to actually go into town by now. Today's goal is to find an inn to stay at, then get myself stocked up on cash and food.

I had a good feeling that the baron's search radius was waaay off the mark. First, I'd made sure to avoid and hide from anyone who looked like they were in a hurry, whether they were on a cart, riding a horse, or otherwise situated. Second, it seemed like my stamina was actually pretty low compared to the denizens of this world, so I thought I'd been moving at a pace much slower than others around my age. No one would think a fugitive on the run would actually be running away *half* as fast as anyone would normally get around— also, I'd already changed the color of my hair and eyes. I was pretty sure I didn't need to be so on guard anymore. I was almost out of food, as well, so I'd still need to go resupply anyway.

Oh yeah… I wondered what the baron was thinking when he saw the empty room I'd left behind. Maybe he thought the whole thing was just incredibly bizarre. Maybe he thought he'd messed with the wrong person, or that it'd be for the best to just forget everything that happened. There was also a possibility that he couldn't forget his one chance at attaining fame and rising up in the ranks of the nobility, or that he convinced himself there was a group of people who had broken into his manor to help bust me out. Who really knew?

Whatever the heck he made of it, I couldn't care less now that I'd finally made it to safety. With that in mind, it was time to head toward the town.

I barely had any money to my name right now. I'd only managed to scrounge up forty bronze coins and four small silver ones back at the guild, after all. That was probably about the same as 400 yen back home, I'd say. I would end up blowing through everything I had if I just, say, bought four meat skewers from a food cart or something…

And, right now, I found myself holding four large skewers in my hands.

""Ah…"

My current savings: a big fat zero. I'd planned ahead for something like this, of course, and made sure to change in the shelter of the trees before going into town.

I was back to wearing the maid outfit from before. Anyone would be suspicious if a commoner like myself came up and tried selling the things I had, *ahem*, "acquired" from the baron's place. There was a pretty good chance they'd suspect these were stolen goods (and they'd be right, but I digress). So you'd think putting on one of the dresses that used to belong to the baron's daughter would be a good idea, right? Maybe pretend to be some rich noble's daughter or something? Wrong. There was no aristocrat dumb enough to send their daughter, ignorant to the ways of the world, to sell some trinkets. That just seemed sketchy, no matter how you sliced it.

And so, my conclusion: the outfit I was now wearing was the least likely to cause anyone to be suspicious of me.

At a certain secondhand shop—

A young maid entered the store, then gingerly approached the owner.

"Um, excuse me, sir... My master told me to sell this so I could go buy food for today..."

She looked up at him with forlorn, puppy-dog eyes, cradling a candlestick in her hands. The shopkeeper's eyes, on the other hand, practically popped out of their sockets.

"Booyah!"

I had six silver coins clenched in my hand. It only cost four coins to spend the night somewhere, including dinner and breakfast. If we assumed it'd cost about four small silver coins for stuff like a towel and hot water to take a bath, then I should have one silver coin and six small ones left to go out and buy food. That should be enough to keep me going when I'd rough it in the wilderness tomorrow, then I'd reach the next town the day after that! All right, it was time to head to the inn.

"That'll be five silver coins for a night's stay with two meals."

Son of a... It seemed big towns meant bigger prices than back out in the sticks.

It'd still be a few days until I could make it to the capital. Right when I was thinking I should be looking for a place to set up camp, I saw a clearing not too far off from the main road that had clean water flowing down from the side of a mountain.

"Hey, this ain't half bad!"

I scooped out some water and used it to wash my face. I could make potions that were like water, but this was the real good stuff if you wanted to wash your face. I could even use it to wash my hands, should nature call.

All right, I'm totally camping here for today! But, that said, a girl like myself can't just sleep in a place you can see from the road. I think I'll head a bit deeper into the forest so all the travelers passing by aren't gawking at me.

After having my fill of using all the clean water I wanted, I pushed my way through the trees to set up camp.

"Are we there yet?"

"Please wait until we can find a place to park the carriage away from the main road," the lady knight in her late twenties said, trying to pacify the ten-year-old girl fidgeting around restlessly in the carriage.

"That's why we told you to go *before* we left..." There was a pointed rebuke from a boy around twelve or thirteen as he rolled his eyes at his little sister.

"But I didn't have to go then..."

This particular kind of carriage was used only by the nobility, and had an entourage of six mounted knights in front of and behind it acting as escorts. There were four passengers currently riding inside of it, including the brother, his sister, and the lady knight from before, as well as a maid. The aristocratic siblings were on their way to visit their grandmother, who had taken ill recently, with the escort of knights accompanying them there.

The little girl had apparently been set upon by the call of nature, and asked for them to stop the carriage so she could go take care of her "business." They told her they couldn't stop in the middle of the road and block off traffic, so they were currently looking for a place to park the carriage.

"There's a spot just up ahead we can stop at!" the knight captain leading the escort shouted back.

Looking into it further, they decided it was indeed a good place to pull off. It was a fairly spacious place, and even had a running stream with fresh water flowing down the side of a mountain. No one would have any complaints washing their hands there. They'd probably cleared the area to make it a rest stop that everyone could use, and the group couldn't be more thankful for that.

With the carriage parked, the girl hastily clambered down from the carriage, and with a short, "I'll come with you too," her brother followed after her.

The captain, lady knight, and brother all headed a little ways into the forest together to accompany the girl. Only the lady knight ended up chaperoning the girl all the way, however. The remaining knights stayed behind to guard the carriage. After all, there was a much higher chance of bandits attacking them back on the road rather than anyone running into danger in such a small forest.

After the girl had finished her business, she walked back with the lady knight to meet up where the guys were waiting. However, the boy and the captain were both staring in a daze at something deeper in the forest. Curious, the two girls got closer to take a look for themselves...

It was there...that they found a goddess.

She laid upon a large bed, enshrined in a small clearing among the trees. Judging by how thick the underbrush was, there was no feasible way such a large bed could have been carried there. There were no nearby indications that suggested it was dragged there, either. Resting on top of the unlikely sleeping arrangements was a young goddess, hair the color of silver, and clothed in a gown of pure white.

The four of them stood there, unable to say a word...until the little girl summoned up all her courage to step forward.

"Y-Yunith!"

The boy tried stopping her, but his little sister paid him no mind and kept walking ahead. When she finally made it just beside the sleeping goddess, she called out to her.

"Miss Goddess... Miss Goddess!"

The goddess slowly opened her eyes, then gracefully turned toward the girl before saying the following:

"Whaddya want?! Shut the hell up!"

"Eek!"

It appeared getting up was harsh for the goddess—just about as harsh as the look in her eyes. It was then more than ever that the girl was glad she had finished her business *before* coming here.

"So you come down here from heaven sometimes to rest?"

"Yes, that's right. That way I can bestow my holy power upon nature's forests like this."

I made up some random BS to answer the little girl's question and prayed from the bottom of my heart that they would just leave me alone already.

I'd pulled out the bed I'd taken from the baron's place to sleep on, and was wearing a white dress as a replacement for actual pajamas. After sprinkling some of my beast-repellant potion everywhere, I was in the middle of getting myself some nice shut-eye...but it looked like I'd overslept a bit. Though I couldn't see it that well, because of all the trees blocking it, it seemed like the sun was already pretty high up in the sky.

"So why would the goddess Celestine be—"

"Oh, I'm not Celes."

"What?!"

Oops. Since they thought I was a goddess, everyone seemed to be in a panic when I said I wasn't Celes, who was supposed to be the one and only *true* goddess of this world. *Welp, guess I better think of something!*

"Actually, I'm a friend of Celes. I came here from another world. She told me I could stay here in her world and enjoy myself."

Well, I wasn't lying.

"Oh, a goddess from another world! Not only that, but an acquaintance of the great Celestine as well..." the guy who looked like a knight exclaimed in surprise.

Well, yeah, can't say I blame him. Guess anyone would react like that after hearing what I just said. But it looks like they actually understand the concept of "other worlds"... Huh, how 'bout that.

I went ahead and listened to what they had to say.

It seemed like the grandmother of the brother and sister had fallen ill, and things weren't looking good. The grandmother had always been so nice to them that they insisted on seeing her, which was why they were traveling with a group of knights to escort them there. It sounded like grandma was an aristocrat who had married early at fifteen and given birth just as early at sixteen. That wasn't a strange thing to hear about in this world, and usually a "grandma" could be a person anywhere between thirty and forty years old. If this grandma already had grandchildren this old, I guessed she was over forty, though.

Anyways, it looked like she wasn't suffering because of old age or anything, but because of an actual disease.

"Goddess, please grant us a blessing for our grandmother..."

That was the plea I heard from the boy.

Hmm... Yeah, sure. Why not? Right now I'm just a nameless, green-eyed, silver-haired goddess to them. Now then, let me think up a good reason to give them my "blessing"...

"Very well. Someone tell me a sad story, if you please."

"...Huh?"

"Exactly what I said: someone tell me a real tear-jerker of a story and make me cry, please."

Any miracle medicine has gotta be made with the "tears of a goddess" or something, right?

Everyone seemed to catch on quickly, and thus began our impromptu "Sad Story Time" competition.

"...and that's how she ended up dumping me..."

Next!

"…which is when Father got absolutely livid with me…"

Nope!

"…it was awful! How could Felicia do that!"

Nuh-uh! Man, these all kinda suck… Maybe I went with the wrong idea?

"Um… I don't think any story I tell will be that interesting, but…"

Last up is the knight lady, huh.

"Back when I was around sixteen or seventeen, I had plenty of gentlemen callers express their interest in me, but I turned them all down to focus solely on my training, so I could become a knight. Right as I finally came to think of myself as a full-fledged knight, that's when I realized my friends and my colleagues had already married and had children. I'm already twenty-seven, my hands are covered in blisters from using my sword, and the muscles I've gained put me as far away as possible from having anything close to a soft, woman-ish body… I've started to wonder if I'm going to be alone my whole life, or that I'll, um, grow old by myself… And, um, when I think about that, I… No, never mind. This isn't something you would care to hear about, I know, but… Wait, whoa!"

And lo, the Goddess wept!

I'm bawling my eyes out here!

I presented them with three potion vials.

"That was so sad, I already made three of these…"

"O-Oh…" The lady knight seemed a little taken aback, as if she didn't seem to think the story she told was *that* sad.

TREES

"Give this blue one to your grandmother," I said as I handed the boy a potion.

"For you, I want you to drink this red one. Just be warned that you may be in trouble if you don't drink this in front of someone everyone really trusts. And your superiors. And maybe whoever you work for as well."

"R-Right…" the lady knight said.

"You can give this last yellow one to whomever you want, so just have whatever sick or injured person you want to heal drink this."

I handed the last potion to the lady knight as well.

I had only picked those colors because I wanted to make the potions easy to tell apart from each other this time around. They didn't have the same effects as the healing potions I made the last time I'd chosen this particular color palette.

"Then you should all be off. I'll be taking my leave from this world soon, and the surge of divine energy from when my bed disappears can have harmful effects on humans. Hurry along now."

I said as much to urge them to get going, and the four of them thanked me profusely before they took their leave. I made sure to threaten them with that whole "divine energy" mumbo jumbo, so I doubted they'd come back to try to take a peek at what I was doing… But, just to be safe, I used the gaps between the trees to watch the carriage and the escort of mounted knights be on their merry way before I did anything else. When they were gone, that was when I got to changing my clothes and packing my bed away before getting the heck out of there. That had eaten up some of my time, but it was actually kinda fun, so I'd say everything worked out fine.

I only had a little farther to go until I reached Brancott's capital.

I may have been a little rash conjuring up those potions, but I doubted anyone would come searching me out if they all thought I was a goddess who just happened to have descended to this world. It wouldn't be strange for those potions to have miraculous effects on them either; everything that happened was "the work of a goddess" after all.

That said, I may have gone a little overboard with the red potion. I didn't know if it'd have the *exact* effects I was thinking of, but I bet that lady knight would be pretty happy as long as it did even a portion of what I tried to make it do. I mean, that story was just too sad. She really made me a blubbering mess back there... I had to make sure I didn't end up like that myself. Let's call the gift I gave her a sort of "tuition fee" for that valuable life lesson *she* ended up giving *me*.

A few months after Kaoru had escaped from Baron Renie—

The nameless girl from the baron's mansion—well, it wasn't like she *really* didn't have a name, of course—but the girl Kaoru had taken the maid outfit from was a girl of little fortune. Kaoru had thought her to be around fifteen or sixteen years old, but that was only because Kaoru had the bad habit of thinking foreigners looked older than they really were. In reality, this girl was only twelve years old. And right now, the girl was in a panic—more panicked than she'd ever been before. After all, the girl had just taken on an enormous debt, since the baron was charging her for the maid outfit that girl who knocked her out had run off with.

While the baron was no saint, it wasn't like he was the very embodiment of all the world's evil or anything. He was just your normal, money-grubbing sleazeball, who loved looking down on commoners. Just your average, everyday aristocrat.

Her maid outfit had been loaned to her by the baron's household. Since it was her fault that it had been stolen, she had to reimburse them for the missing clothes. It wasn't an unreasonable request by any means; in fact, you could even say she was lucky she got off with only being yelled at for letting the girl escape, and not having them demand she compensate them for everything that was taken from that room. It seemed even the baron wasn't that much of a horrible excuse for a human being.

However, the outfits used for maids working in noble households were expensive. Like, "almost costs a small fortune" expensive. That's why they were provided free of charge instead of being paid for out of pocket by the maids. Now, she had to work to send money back home, so she could only repay her debts a little at a time. As of now, she'd barely even made a dent in paying off that debt. At this rate, who knew how long it would take to pay the whole thing off... Just thinking about it was enough to sap away what hope she had left.

The girl was looking all gloom and doom as usual today, and while her fellow maids felt sorry for her, their hands were tied. Just like the girl, everyone else was also sending what money they earned back home to their families, and they didn't have the luxury of sparing any for her.

It was then the head maid called out to the girl, "A package arrived addressed to you, so come pick it up later."

After her work was finished, the girl collected her package and went back to her room. It wasn't actually her *own* room, however. It was a room made for four people, with two bunk beds. The other three maids just hadn't come back yet.

The name on the package said it was sent by a "Kaoru," but she had no clue who that could be. It was definitely addressed to her, though, and she couldn't return it. There was no address for the sender, and she didn't have the money to send it back, either. Reluctantly, she opened the package.

"Ah…"

Inside was the maid uniform that had been taken from her. Not only that, but there was another smaller, carefully packaged box tucked away inside the bigger one. When she opened that as well, she found a small bottle filled with some sort of strange liquid, and a letter that came with it.

I'm sorry for before. I'm returning the clothes I ended up borrowing from you. Make sure to drink everything inside the bottle as soon as you read this, so it isn't stolen from you, and I recommend you don't speak of it to anyone.

—Kaoru

The girl was utterly bewildered. She was angry toward the girl who stole her outfit, then she was overjoyed having it back so she wouldn't be in debt anymore. And then, she was *tremendously* doubtful about this suspicious liquid.

With all these thoughts whirling around inside the girl's head, she just stopped thinking and downed the contents of the bottle—all at once.

"M-Mmph… That…was pretty good…"

"I heard you got your outfit back. Thank goodness, right?"

"Yeah, the person who took it sent it back here! I'm saved!"

The other maids were celebrating the fact that a smile had finally returned to the girl's face.

"So I can tell you're feeling a lot better now, but aren't you kind of, I dunno...*too* happy?"

"Huh? You think so?"

The girl tried feigning ignorance, but there was obviously something up with her. Her hair was glossy and smooth, her cheeks soft as silk, and her hands showed no signs of wear and tear from work whatsoever. She had actually been constipated until yesterday, due to all the stress, so there was no way she would suddenly start acting like this now.

"Did something happen?"

"Nope, nothing at all. I've never felt better, now that I'm debt-free, and I even got back the money I already paid, too! I bet all that happiness I'm feeling is just showing up on the outside now!"

"Seems a bit fishy if you ask me..."

"Ehehe..."

Not long after, rumors of an "angel" spread not only among the maids in the mansion, but to the neighboring countries as well. But there wasn't a single person who connected those rumors with the commoner girl who'd been held at the mansion for all of one day... Well, except for maybe *one* person. And right before she went to bed that day, the young girl offered another prayer of gratitude, just like she always did.

"Thank you again for everything, Kaoru, the angel sent by the goddess Celestine herself..."

Chapter 4:
The Royal Capital

Grua, the royal capital of the Kingdom of Balmore—

A family of nobles was kneeling in the throne room of the royal palace.

"Raise your heads."

The nobles lifted themselves up at the command of the young king, a man who appeared to be in his mid-twenties.

Gerald von Adan was the current head of the Adan household, which was the family of aristocrats who had an audience with the king today. Behind him were his eldest son and eldest daughter, both of whom were still children: Hector, and his little sister, Yunith. Also with them were the captain of the knights who guarded them, Robert, and the lady knight, Francette. Also present in the throne room were the king's ministers, other members of the upper echelons of nobility, and a great number of those with a higher social status.

"So, Earl Adan, would these be the people who claim to have met the goddess?"

The king looked especially amused as he asked his question. Earl Adan, in turn, respectfully gave his answer.

"That is correct, Your Majesty. It happened when my wife's mother was suffering from illness, and my children were on their way to visit her... Robert was the captain in charge of the knights accompanying them, and he insisted they share the details."

"If I remember correctly, your wife was raised in Brancott, was she not? Very well, I shall allow him to answer directly. Robert, speak your piece."

After receiving permission from the king, Robert explained what he'd experienced during his time as captain of the escort.

"Hmm… Seems like quite the tall tale, if you ask me."

The king let out a wry chuckle, and snickers could be heard coming from the other nobility in attendance, causing Robert's face to turn red.

"And? What happened after that?"

"My king, we delivered the medicine we'd received from the goddess to the grandmother, and the moment she drank it… Why, she made a complete recovery."

"As if anyone would believe such trite…" "What are they plotting?" "They dare deceive the king?"

An almost indescribable atmosphere fell over the throne room, filled with scorn from all the others in attendance. At this rate, the Adan household would be marked as liars and made into a laughingstock.

Just as that thought was passing through everyone's minds, the lady knight Francette suddenly spoke up.

"Your Majesty, please look at this!"

Taking a yellow vial of medicine from her breast pocket, she offered it to the king. He hesitated for a moment, but then gave his order.

"Bring it here."

One of the king's retainers fetched the medicine and handed it over to the king, who squinted his eyes as he scrutinized it.

"This is the medicine of the goddess, then?"

"Yes. Please, give that to Sir Roland."

"What?! Oh, I see now... *This* is the reason you requested my brother be here today."

Roland, the brother of King Serge. A military genius with an aptitude for politics, he'd earned the trust of all those who served under him. Ever since he was a child, everyone had believed that he was going to make a wonderful king in the future. However, misfortune befell him when he took on grievous wounds trying to protect his brother Serge, the current king. Because of that, he'd lost the ability to move his right arm.

Roland had given up his place as heir and relinquished his claim to the throne to his younger brother. When their father passed away, he worked as a mighty pillar of support for his brother after Serge took the crown. There was no one Serge trusted more, or was more grateful toward, than Roland, and the guilt Serge felt from what had transpired haunted him to this day.

"Cease this at once!" a voice shouted out from among the nobles, "You cannot have Sir Roland drink such a dubious concoction!"

At that time, Francette had already risen to her feet. Standing up completely straight, she took out another bottle of medicine from her breast pocket and lifted it high above her head. Red filled the inside of the bottle.

"This medicine has been gifted to me by the goddess herself! Behold, my king!"

Please let this work, Goddess!

Francette pulled the cap from the bottle and downed its contents all at once. The lady knight's body was suddenly enveloped in a bright light, and the next moment...

"Ohhhhhh!"

"Wh-Whaaat?!"

Standing before them was the lady knight—but now with smoother, glossier skin, and a slightly smaller frame than she'd had just moments ago. The armor she wore was now loose, and, no matter how you looked at her, she had the appearance of a girl who was fifteen or sixteen years old.

Ignoring the commotion among the other nobles, the king grabbed the yellow potion and ran over to his brother.

"Roland, drink this!"

"No, you should save it should something ever happen to you..."

Roland tried pushing away his little brother with his left hand, but Serge wouldn't back down.

"You heard what these people have said! The goddess told this knight to give this to whoever she saw fit!" Serge was on the verge of tears as he continued. "She chose you... This medicine is for you, Roland!"

Looking at his little brother's face, Roland knew Serge wouldn't give up. He gave in to Serge's pleas and took the bottle. Taking off the cap in silence, he slowly drank what was inside. For a moment, nothing seemed to be happening. His body didn't start glowing, and he didn't suddenly become younger.

However—

"I... I can move it..."

"Roland!"

"My right arm... It's moving..."

Serge was overcome with emotion at seeing Roland being able to move his arm freely again, embracing him as tears streamed down. Roland returned his little brother's embrace, tears flowing just as freely from his eyes. The nobles who'd been raising such a fuss fell silent, the sight of the two brothers holding each other bringing tears to their own eyes.

"Roland, let's hurry and conduct your coronation. That way you can finally become king…"

"No, no…"

"…Wh-What?" King Serge was speechless after his brother so casually turned down the throne.

"Being king is such a pain, and I'm not going to let you push all of that on me. I'll leave such annoyances up to you, so I can enjoy a more carefree life!"

"R-Roland, you…"

Francette was trembling from pure joy. A younger body! It was lean and fit, but not to the point where she was a solid chunk of muscle, and boasted skin that was smooth as silk. She was twenty-seven years old on record, but if the goddess made her sixteen, then she could say she was sixteen now, loud and proud! She was a little sad over losing the strength and endurance she worked so hard to build up, but it wasn't like she'd forgotten everything she'd learned or anything. Since she didn't have to commit as much time to training, she would have plenty of time to spend with the gentlemen callers who came to see her now.

Heh… Heheh…

"Hey, can you *not* laugh to yourself with that creepy look on your face?"

"Quiet, you!"

Just when she was enjoying her newfound happiness, her captain had to butt in and ruin the moment. She gave him a hefty shove, making sure to put extra *oomph* into it since her body was a bit weaker now.

OOF!

Her right hand sent the captain flying away much faster—and way farther—than she'd been expecting. He crashed and skid along the ground after being blasted off his feet.

"...Huh?"

Um... It doesn't actually seem like my speed or strength has dropped at all... Actually, did I get stronger?

"You said you were Francette, the knight, correct?"

"Y-Yes!" She jumped in surprise after Roland suddenly began speaking to her.

"I know for a fact we haven't met face-to-face before...so why me?"

"What?"

"Like I said, I'm asking why you chose to use that medicine on me. It's not like you're in service to the royal family or anything."

"W-Well, erm... That's because, um..."

She couldn't say it... She couldn't say how she'd admired him for all these years. She'd fallen for him after seeing how brave he was protecting his little brother, and it was because of him she'd worked so hard to go from an attendant to a noble family to officially becoming a knight. That was why it was her dream to one day be in service to the royal family themselves, but she couldn't say that... She wasn't some starry-eyed fifteen- to sixteen-year-old girl or anything.

"Well, that's fine for now. I'll be asking you the details *personally* later though."

"H-Huh...?"

I'd finally made it. Here I was in Aras, the capital of Brancott. Luckily for me, a merchant who just happened to pass me by this morning let me ride in his wagon. He was on the way back from selling his wares, and there was plenty of space in the cart, since he hadn't picked up too much stuff wherever he'd been doing business. The wagon also wasn't in a huge rush to get wherever they were going, so it wasn't like it was supersonic fast compared to walking.

Either way, I'd say it was about twice as fast as it was going on foot. But that was only compared to an adult male in this world. Compared to my walking speed, this was at least five times as fast (my frequent breaks aside). Now I wouldn't have to wear myself out traveling...though it did make my butt sore. Thanks to this, though, I'd made it to the capital by the afternoon, which was way faster than what I'd been planning on.

The reason the merchant picked me up in the first place wasn't *just* because he was worried about seeing a small child who looked dead tired as she walked by herself. The merchant's son was also in the back of the wagon, and seemed pretty bored from the trip, so the merchant was hoping I could keep him company and chat with him—and chat with him I did.

He was only about ten years old, so he wasn't much good for figuring out what the deal was with this world. He said he wanted to follow in his father's footsteps and get into the trade as well, so I taught him a few tricks to get by in business, as well as how to handle customers. Basically, I drilled the type of customer service they had in Japan into him. I took no responsibility for anything that happened because of that, though.

In exchange, he taught me all about the geography around here. I was shocked, frankly, at just how much he knew about the surrounding countries and what their relationships were with each other, despite how young he was. I guess I should have expected that sort of knowledge from a merchant's son.

According to what he had to say, the Kingdom of Brancott (the country we were in now) was located around the base of a peninsula sticking out to the west from the continent, with four more countries located just beyond it. Of the two countries sharing a border with Brancott, the Kingdom of Balmore lay to the north, while the Kingdom of Aseed lay to the south, and both were stable monarchies. Even further to the west of those two, located on the very tip of the peninsula, was a militaristic nation headed by a dictatorship: the Aligot Empire. Now, there was also a range of steep mountains that separated the two kingdoms from the Aligot Empire. It wasn't anything that couldn't be climbed over, as long as you tried hard enough, but since the only other route available was a long detour by boat, it acted as an inhibitor for trade between them all.

The last nation worth mentioning was the Holy Land of Rueda, a religious state located on the coastline just northwest of Balmore. The country shared a border with the Aligot Empire, but possessed very little military might, on account of being a fairly small country. Putting it as simply as possible, imagine the Tohoku region of Japan (or look it up), but flipped ninety degrees to the left. Aomori would be where the Aligot Empire was at, Iwate being the kingdom of Balmore, Akita being the Kingdom of Aseed, and Yamagata and Miyagi combined would be the kingdom of Brancott. If you wanted to head to the continent itself from any of those countries, you would need to pass through Brancott first.

The capital of Brancott was actually located a good deal west of the center of the country, while Balmore's capital was the opposite, located farther to the east. The two countries were on friendly terms with each other, and the locations of their capitals made them feel even closer together, but in the literal sense of the word. Well, "close" as far as this world was concerned, anyway.

The merchant was nice enough to buy three of the "going-away presents" I had snagged from the baron's mansion. I made a big show of making it look like I was taking it out of a bag I already had on me, of course. He told me it was going to be a bit less than I'd get at any of the proper shops, but I was more than happy to sell them. Now I wouldn't have to worry about inn fees for the next few days.

I had him drop me off in front of the city gates, expressed my thanks to him, and then we parted ways. Unlike the merchant and his son, who had proof of citizenship and a card showing they were registered merchants, I was a fresh, new arrival. It looked like there were still some hoops to jump through before they would let me in.

As you might expect from the royal capital, it was a completely walled-off city, and anyone trying to get in had to pass through a gate under protection from the guards posted at it. I was directed to wait in a different line, since I was a new arrival, which was when we ended up playing the "What business do you have here?" game. Maybe a young girl all by herself was too suspicious, after all.

"Now why are you all alone? Where's your family?"

The soldier attacks!

"They're all dead... My uncle stole the house and land my father had left me, then tried to sell me off as a slave as well. That's why I ran away by myself... I thought I might find someone to work for in the city so I can get by..."

I strike back. The soldier takes a mortal blow!

He took care of the rest of my paperwork right away. He said he was sorry to ask, but new arrivals needed to pay three silver coins to finish the process, but I was more than set, thanks to the merchant buying my stuff earlier.

After getting myself a temporary entry pass, I was told I needed to find myself some actual work if I wanted to get an official pass. I was already planning on doing that from the beginning, of course. I was going to get myself a job while figuring out more about this world. I'd decided I wasn't going to sell any more of my healing potions. At most, I would only use them on myself from now on.

I might be able to sell other stuff as long as I don't make it too valuable. Maybe something like good ol' sodium chloride... No, no, bad idea. Salt is bad. It's too dangerous to try anything when I don't know how widely distributed it is, or how much it sells for, or even if there's a monopoly on it or something. Nope, not making the same mistake I did with potions again... Gotta live and learn, me.

After finally getting through the gates, I began heading toward the place that was supposed to help you get work, which the merchant was kind enough to tell me about. If I didn't find a good job right away, I'd be sleeping at the inn tonight. If anyone was hiring that'd let me live in-house with them, then my plan was to head over to check it out ASAP.

Unlike the Hunter's Guild, where mercenaries and soldiers would take on the dangerous jobs like hunting quests and the more perilous gathering missions, the job-hunting agency was a place where you could find much more normal lines of work. This was the place where the agency could find you jobs working at a store or as a hired hand, all sorts of unskilled labor, or even safe and simple gathering quests. The employer would fill out a request application and pay a fee to have it put up. Once they found someone they wanted to hire, they would next have to pay a finders' fee to the agency, since the ones applying to take these requests usually didn't have much money in the first place. Even if the person they hired quit immediately after being hired, there were no refunds. They'd picked out the person themselves, and the agency wouldn't hesitate to point that out if they tried saying anything.

After I made my way to the job-hunting agency, I went ahead and checked out the details for the help-wanted requests posted on the board. I looked a bunch of them over, but there were all sorts of extra requirements I couldn't compromise on, such as location, type of work, their terms for hiring someone; stuff like that. There was one job that was in some far-off mountains, another one that was all heavy-lifting, one that was for guys only, and another one where you needed prior experience…

I couldn't pick one that took up too much of my free time, either, since it would interfere with me going out to gather more information about where I was. I was fine with them taking money out of my paycheck, as long as I got a place to stay out of it, but working as a maid in a noble's mansion didn't seem like I'd have much "me" time. I tried applying for a job at a bar, but the lady receptionist turned me down, saying it wasn't something minors could apply for. No matter how many times I told her I was fifteen, she just told me it wasn't good to lie, no matter how much I wanted a job. It would've been perfect for finding out more about this world, and I probably could've made a good bit of cash off tips too…

In the end, I was finally hired as a live-in waitress at a restaurant in town. I'd be completely free to do whatever I wanted outside of my shifts, so that worked for me. It even came with meals included, and you shouldn't think I wasn't grateful to hear that.

"Though it may be a little late for this now, how about we take a break for lunch?"

After finally reaching a place to stop in the mountains of paperwork, the Crown Prince of Brancott, Fernand Brancott, let out a long sigh at Fabio's words.

Fabio was the son of the kingdom's prime minister, and, along with Allan, the son of another minister, had been friends with Fernand since they were kids. It wasn't like they all just happened to become friends by chance, though. Their parents had decided it was best for them to be together, and their relationship started off as something like the one you would have with a classmate at school. Though, even though their parents had been the reason that they had met each other, the three of them actually got along quite well. Before they knew it, they'd actually become true friends.

Unlike Fabio, who just seemed like the spitting image of what a prime minister's son should look like, Allan was more like a rugged hunter you'd find in the rougher parts of town. Though he was skilled with a sword, there were parts of him that just didn't seem to fit the noble lifestyle at all. It never crossed their parents' minds that Allan would turn out this way, but Fernand and Fabio liked that about him.

The boys had already turned eighteen, and already had marriage proposals falling into their laps. As the next in line for the throne, Fernand also had to worry about potential candidates to be the royal consort on top of all that. That said, they were all at the age where they just wanted to mess around and have fun.

"Finally… Are you guys eating in your rooms, or should we just have them bring it here?"

"No, Allan and I were thinking of going into town to grab something to eat."

Fernand already knew Allan went out into town often, since he didn't like food at the castle, but it was a rare event for Fabio to go along with him as well. As Fernand thought that, he had an idea.

"All right, I'm coming too."

"I don't know if that's a good idea…"

Talking down the bewildered Fabio, Fernand got to work getting his outfit together so he could travel incognito into town.

"This is it. The food's good, but it's also a pretty cool place in general."

This was a restaurant Allan had been coming to recently, and had invited Fabio to see it for himself. Fernand and Fabio were hesitant at first to enter a commoner's establishment, but there was no way they could back out now—and that went double for Fernand. Fernand had been so insistent on tagging along and now he couldn't embarrass Allan by refusing to go.

When the group went inside, they found the restaurant fairly devoid of customers, mostly since the lunchtime rush had passed. It didn't seem strange for them to be taking last calls for lunch orders any moment now.

Allan picked a table at random to sit down at, then showed the other two the menu.

"Take a look at the stuff they have down on the bottom-right. It's all pretty interesting."

When Fernand and Fabio took a look for themselves, they found a variety of dishes listed there…or what they assumed to be dishes at least.

"'Big and Soft Soup Pasta,' 'Soup Rice, Plum or Salmon Edition,' 'T(omato) C(hicken) R(ice) E(gg) Wraps'… What the heck *is* all this?"

Fabio was flabbergasted by all this cuisine he'd never heard of before.

"You can just leave that part to me. 'Scuse me! Three orders of TCRE wraps over here, please!"

"Ah, hey! Don't just decide for us…"

Allan went ahead and ordered for the table, though the looks on the other two's faces seemed less than happy about that.

After waiting a bit for the waitress to bring the food to the table, Allan asked her a question.

"Hey, Aimee, do you think we could get some advice today?"

"Sure thing. The only people you have ahead of you are that parent and his kid, so it should be fine. What kinda course you goin' for?"

"How about we go with five silver coins today?"

"Whoa, look at Mr. Generous over here! Thanks a bunch!"

The waitress they'd been talking to, Aimee, looked in pretty high spirits as she walked away.

"What was up with that just now… What are you trying to pull, Allan?"

"That's just something you can look forward to finding out! Anyway, you better eat before your food gets cold!"

Though the other two were plenty suspicious over what Allan was up to, they both dug into their meals.

"Huh?"

The two were in shock after taking a bite of their food. Their hands stopped for just an instant before digging in with added gusto. Their spoons were practically a blur as they ate.

"Whaddya think? Pretty good stuff, right? Just goes to show you can't underestimate commoner restaurants!"

"You're right. You went out of your way to bring us here for it, after all."

Fabio had no retort to Allan's smug look of satisfaction. But still, Allan kept a mischievous look on his face.

"What are you talking about? I know the food is good and all, but I wouldn't bring the ever-busy Sir Fabio all the way down here for just *that*."

Fabio had a blank look on his face, like he didn't understand what was going on. Fernand seemed keen to know the details, but kept quiet while watching the two of them talk.

"I think they should just be about done taking orders now."

Right after Allan said that, a girl appeared from the kitchen and headed over to the merchant family sitting near their table. She looked to be about eleven or twelve years old, and had black hair and eyes, which was a little unusual to see around here. The way her face looked seemed to suggest she came from a foreign country. She was cute, there was no doubt about that, and she looked like an intellectual to boot. It was just…the look in her eyes was a little on the harsh side. Actually, *way* on the harsh side, to be honest. Children who were faint of heart probably wouldn't want to get within five meters of her, it was so bad.

She'd killed *at least* four or five people. That was how bad the look in her eyes was.

"That's Kaoru, the girl I wanted to show you today."

"Her?"

Allan gave a wide grin after seeing how surprised Fabio was. "Yup, once they stop taking orders, it frees up some time for the other waitresses. After the manager gives the okay, that's when it turns into a sort of counseling center. All the other waitresses get a cut of the profits, so they all seem pretty happy to take on whatever work is left from whoever is doing the counseling."

The girl had made it to the table next to them by the time he finished saying that. The three of them pricked up their ears and listened in on the conversation.

"Thanks for always stopping by, Bohman. What did you want advice on today?"

"Actually, it's not me asking the questions today, but my son Charles. Seems like he has something he wanted to ask you about."

"Five small silver coins should be enough to cover that then. All right, Charles, let's hear it."

Despite the harsh look in her eyes, having a cute girl smile at him caused the ten-year-old boy to blush slightly as he asked his question.

"Um, it's what we talked about last time... About customers who come to complain. They make up such a small portion of all the customers you get, so wouldn't it be best to forget about them and treat the other not-rude customers better instead? Then you wouldn't have to go out of your way to deal with those kinds of people, and you wouldn't have to practice how to work it out with them... Isn't it all just a big waste of time otherwise?"

The girl answered the young boy's question with a smile, the scary look in her eyes replaced with something a little more gentle.

"Actually, it turns out there are tons of people who won't go out of their way to complain to you, even if they're not satisfied about something. Instead of dragging themselves all the way to the store to complain, they can just move on to the next place. Just because they don't come to complain doesn't mean they're all satisfied customers. People like that won't go to the store to complain, but will tell other people instead. When they do, the people running the store will start seeing fewer customers without knowing why. But, among all those customers, there are some who will take the time to tell you about the parts of your store that need improving. Wouldn't you be grateful to have people as kind as them do that for you?"

"Ah..."

"Still, there are some people who are just trying to get money out of you by making up nonexistent problems. You have to make sure to never give them money, even if you think parting with a bit of cash is worth avoiding the issue altogether. If rumor spreads that your shop will just give up money when pressured, you'll get all sorts of unsavory types coming to extort you. You have to be firm and hold your ground against those people, even if it means a loss of profits on your end."

"Got it."

"Also, don't you think customers would be happy to see a shop take their advice seriously and put it into practice? Happy enough that they would want to *continue* giving them their patronage. Catch my drift?"

"Y-Yeah, that's true..."

"Listen, Charles. Customers aren't just suckers for merchants to take money from; they're people you do business with on fair terms. They can be friends, and they can be teachers with tons to teach you."

"I see..."

The girl continued her explanation, and there was an expression of admiration on the father's face as he listened intently as well.

Who is that girl?! Fabio whispered, *Rather, what is that girl?!*
Pretty cool, right? Allan replied.
This is way beyond it being "cool" or not!

You get all that for five small silver coins? Fernand interjected, *Didn't you say five whole silver coins earlier, Allan?*

I'll let you do the asking, Fabio, so think nice and hard about what you wanna make it about.

Wh-What are you saying all of—

She appeared.

"I heard you're going for five silver coins today, Allan? Aimee was back over there doing the 'money makin' mamba.'"

What type of dance is that?!

"Well, as you can see, I came here with some friends today. This one's Fernie, and the other one's Fabie. This guy said he had something he wanted to ask, right?" Allan said, passing the baton to Fabio.

"U-Uh..."

Fabio was in full-on panic mode as he desperately tried coming up with a question.

Kaoru had a second job she worked between shifts as a waitress—with the blessing of her manager and fellow waitresses, of course. That job was running a sort of counseling service. She would listen to whatever questions her clients had, then answer those questions and give them advice. She only had a short time to run it, since the only free time she had as a waitress was after the call for last orders was finished.

It cost a pretty penny to even get inside the library, and trying to buy a book was basically a pipe dream here. That's when Kaoru decided to open up her counseling service, since she was trying to save up every little bit she could. Being able to talk with a whole rainbow of people could end up being pretty useful too, after all.

When she was running her counseling service, her fellow waitresses would have to take on whatever work she had left over, which was why she was giving them a forty percent cut of what she made. If two people ended up covering her, then they would get twenty percent each, and so on and so forth. If they were lucky enough to hit upon a customer with deep pockets like Allan, that meant they were getting one silver coin a piece. The girls weren't exactly making money hand over fist as waitresses, so this definitely wasn't an amount to be sneezed at. They were so over the moon about it that they'd start doing the "money makin' mamba."

Kaoru had learned her lesson from last time, and she wasn't going to start selling anything; she was going to be a clever girl and use her wits to make her money. Her job even came with a place to stay, and food on top of that, so she was in no rush to amass her savings.

Of course, no one wanted to take Kaoru up on her counseling venture at first. After all, who would come to a girl who looked to be about eleven or twelve and tell her all their troubles, or ask for advice? The advertisement hung near the corner of the wall would just look down glumly at Kaoru...

But one day, she reached a turning point. Maybe it was just because he wanted someone to talk to, but a middle-aged man had asked for Kaoru's services. Not only did he pay the counseling fee of five small silver coins (about 500 yen), but he even treated her to something to drink as well. His problem was that he wanted to pass on his business to his two grandchildren, but no matter how he tried splitting up the work between them, they always said it was unfair. The man's son had already passed away, and he just didn't want there to be any bad blood between his grandchildren.

Piece of cake! I've heard of this before! was the first thing Kaoru thought after hearing him out.

"Well, first you should ask one of them how they would split the work to make it fair. Afterward, you ask the other one to pick which split of the work that the first grandkid divvied up they want to do, and I don't think either of them should have any complaints about it."

The man stared blankly back at Kaoru. Kaoru's fellow waitresses and the customers who all just happened to overhear her first-ever job were also staring at her in shock.

"So that's how you'd do it…"

When news of her first job spread, Kaoru started getting a slow influx of customers, half of whom were messing around with her, and half of whom were seriously asking for advice. There were some who just wanted to do nothing more than sit and chat with Kaoru, but a customer was still a customer. It cost a minimum of five small silver coins to use her service, with no limit on how much the price could go up. There were times Kaoru would decide how much a session would cost, depending on the topic, and there were other times the customer would name their price, and Kaoru would tell them only what she thought was appropriate for that amount.

"There are two villages arguing over which one of their sacred trees is bigger than the other, and they can't climb up to measure them…"

"Measure the length of their shadows at the same time of day."

"I'm trying to figure out which of these has the larger volume: this wooden Goddess statue, or this iron one…"

"Just submerge them in water and measure the… Wait, why do you want to know that in the first place?"

"My boyfriend cheated on me…"

"Break up with him."

Over time, it finally got to the point where customers like Allan would come to ask for her services.

I had two of my regulars coming in to ask me for advice today: Bohman and Allan. Allan looked like the son of some merchant mogul whose business had collapsed or something, but he dressed like a hunter. At first, he would only ask me things half-jokingly, but now we've gotten to the point where he regularly asks me questions and advice on serious things. Allan was a generous customer with deep pockets, and my fellow waitresses Aimee and Agathe were practically jumping for joy when he came. They were already dancing that "money makin' mamba" thing they'd made up earlier.

It looked like Allan was being extra-generous today, since he was putting down a whole *five* silver coins. I wondered if he was just showing off since he was with his friends?

After finishing up the request from Charles, the son of the merchant who'd been kind enough to give me a lift to the capital (definitely got a good feeling Charles was going to make a great merchant someday), I headed over to where Allan and his friends were sitting.

"So, what do you want to ask about?"

Allan's friend Fabie seemed a little flustered when he heard me ask that. He took a second to try to get his thoughts in order, then finally asked me a question. I thought the reason they called me over in the first place was because they wanted advice on something?

"W-Well, um… I was just wondering what the nobility could do to increase the tax revenue they get from their territories."

I couldn't say I was expecting that one, but I pulled myself together and asked a question of my own.

"What angle are we talking about here? Agriculture? Trade? Maybe a place that has some industry going for it? Also, are you looking for long- or short-term gains, or something else entirely?"

Fabie didn't seem to be expecting these types of questions from my end. After hesitating a second, he gave his answer.

"Let's see… How about the fastest way to expect returns for just your plain old, completely average territory?"

"Hmm." I thought it over for a bit before answering the question. "That's a bit much to cover for five silver coins… But I'll do it specially for you, since Allan is the one who brought you in. First, you have to lower taxes. You want to get them down about twenty to thirty percent lower for all your merchants and farmers."

"What? But doesn't that mean less tax revenue?" Fernie suddenly butted into the conversation with his own two cents.

"If you're just taxing them to the point they can barely get by, then that's all you're going to get. But what do you think happens when you *lower* taxes?"

"You get less money from taxes," Fernie gave his best impression of a broken record and said the same thing again.

"On the contrary. If taxes go down, you end up with a surplus on your hands. Farmers can use that extra bit of money they saved to buy better tools, like iron hoes or sharper scythes. Those improved tools mean farming becomes more efficient, and the farmers now end up with a surplus of time on their hands. They can use that time to do things like gathering edible plants from the mountains, making art or handicrafts at home, and all sorts of other things. They'll suddenly find themselves with much more free time on their hands."

"While that sounds great for the farmers, that just means less tax yields for the city, though." This time, Fabie was the one cutting in.

"I'm not finished yet. The taxes on the merchants should be lower at this point too, right? From what I've heard, it seems like territories have all sorts of taxes they charge merchants: taxes for bringing goods in, sales tax for anything sold, and even a tax for taking merchandise out of the territory. But let's say you have one territory where the taxes are incredibly low compared to everywhere else. Which territory do you think a merchant on their way to the capital would want to go through?"

"Ah..."

"Though taxes may be lower by about twenty percent, what happens when you get twice the number of merchants coming through? Or even *three* times as many? On the other hand, what would happen if taxes were higher than the other territories around it? Do you think they'd get more revenue from those taxes?"

"..."

"That would make sales tax within that territory cheap as well. The people living there wouldn't only have more flexibility in their lives, but would have more buying power as well. Any merchant would love to sell their wares in a place like that, especially since they wouldn't have to pay any import or export taxes for anything they'd already sold off. The more they sell, the emptier their carts become, and you can't make money off an empty cart. They'd want to try replenishing some of their stock somehow, even if it means a smaller profit margin than bringing it in themselves. And then, oh, what's this? It seems like there's a ton of handicrafts these farmers made themselves! Buying these on the cheap means that I don't have to pay as much in taxes on them either... You see what I'm getting at?"

The three of them just stared at me with their mouths open... *What's up with them? Oh well.* Anyway, I'd say I'd done enough to cover what they paid.

"Going the agriculture route isn't exactly the *fastest* way, like you asked, but I guess this is enough to cover five silver coins, right?"

"Th-That's plenty…"

"Just who *was* that girl?!"

"Uh… A waitress who works at a restaurant in town?"

"…"

The three guys were talking about Kaoru after having made their way back to the castle. As of yet, governors may have thought about just how far they could raise taxes, but none had thought of lowering taxes on their citizens when they were already low enough for them to get by. It had always been said that only the most talented of governors could find the exact amount at which to set taxes without pushing the people past their breaking point.

That young girl had laughed off that way of thinking as if it were nothing. How could anyone have such knowledge and wisdom at an age like that…

Of course, her suggestion was something that couldn't quite work in reality. Any plan to draw in merchants to a certain territory would just be pulling profits away from the other territories under the kingdom's control. The total tax revenue from all those territories would just go down by however much taxes were lowered, which meant smaller net profits for the country. Besides, if anyone began siphoning profits from a neighboring territory, there was no doubt it'd lead to a flood of complaints and disputes. Her idea was more than enough for getting results as fast as possible though, just like Fabio had asked. Something like this had just never been taken into political consideration on a national level. She had to have a terrifying amount of talent to come up with that at her age.

"I just noticed something…" Fabio started.

"What's up?" Fernand asked back.

"That girl was saying five silver coins would only get us that much, and how agriculture wasn't the fastest way to go about it, right?"

"Uh-huh."

"So let's say we ask her to go over agriculture again, but pay her even more, like, say...five small gold coins? What do you think she would tell us then?"

"Whoa..."

"It makes you want more of her, right?"

"Yeah, definitely more..." Allan chimed in.

"Wha... She's still just a young girl!" Fernand chided.

"Not like that!"

Around that same time, the waitresses of the restaurant were busy raising a toast to Kaoru (with tea of course). They were, after all, getting one whole silver coin out of the deal.

They rarely got much from tips from their commoner patrons, and working at a fairly cheap restaurant meant the waitresses had fairly meager wages to match—and here they were getting a silver coin each without even doing anything. It was safe to say they were grateful to Kaoru for that. *Incredibly* grateful.

"Hm-hm-hm! Even without cheats, this is easy peasy!"

Kaoru was feeling pretty full of herself. She was so full of herself, in fact, that she forgot that having an adult's brain with modern-day knowledge while looking like a child was a pretty big cheat in and of itself.

Chapter 5:
Getting It All Out There

"He's back again…" I muttered, furrowing my eyebrows.

That Fernie guy Allan had brought in before had been showing up here more often lately. He'd always show up right when things were getting busy, calling me over to his table to ask me a whole bunch of questions out of nowhere. If he kept this up, my boss wasn't going to let me run my counseling service anymore. I mean, I was only supposed to do it during the off times, when the crowd had thinned out. It wasn't like Aimee and Agathe could run the restaurant by themselves during rush hour. Allan knew the rules, so why not this guy…

Right now, that troublesome customer was staring straight at me while slurping up a bowl of Big and Soft Soup Noodles (one of the dishes I got the restaurant to officially put on the menu—it's udon, by the way). His hair was a nice shade of blond, and it was true that he didn't look half-bad… Still, my only thoughts on him were as follows:

What a creep…

Prince Fernand had become very, *very* interested in Kaoru, and would frequently come to the restaurant to watch her work. It wasn't like he was the king (yet), so as long as he didn't slack off too much and let work pile up, he didn't have much to do in the first place.

For some reason, Fernand wouldn't invite Fabio along, having snuck out to the restaurant all alone, and Allan had gone back to his hometown the other day, meaning he was out of the picture for now.

While it wasn't as if Fernand was completely ignorant of the ways of the world, the concept of not bothering other people was foreign to him. Being the prince, there was no one around him who had work that took priority over him. It was due to this that he simply forgot why Allan had taken them to the restaurant way past the lunch rush, despite Allan specifically mentioning only going after the last order was called and the waitresses had less work to deal with. People were meant to work themselves around his schedule. To Fernand, that was just common sense—and that was exactly why he committed faux pas after faux pas.

He would call for Kaoru when the restaurant was packed. Even when Kaoru had other people ahead of him for counseling, he would push his way ahead of them so he could see her first. His questions began heading into territory that Kaoru didn't want to talk about, like asking her for more personal information.

At first, Kaoru had made sure to handle it as well as any person would. He was a friend of Allan's after all, so she put up with him. She diligently answered all his questions on policies for the country, even though she couldn't tell if he was testing or messing with her. But Fernand's questions and actions began escalating over time, getting to the point where Kaoru couldn't even answer them anymore. He was even beginning to cause trouble for the other customers, as well.

There was a limit to these sorts of things. It was true that he paid well, but the way he was going about it made it seem like he was saying Kaoru should do anything for him, as long as he gave her money for it, and that attitude was ticking her off. Even when he threw in a gold coin to show off, it only put her more on guard.

Finally, Kaoru went to her boss to ask him for a favor. The manager and the other employees already knew Kaoru was having trouble with Fernand, which was how she received permission to give him a specific reply...

"I'm sorry, but I can no longer be your waitress, Fernie. If you need to order anything, please ask one of the *other* staff."

The next day, Fernand went out of his way to ignore that Agathe was right near him and called Kaoru over, and such was her response. It was practically written on the other customers' faces that they were all waiting for this to happen.

A blank expression hung on Fernand's face, as if he couldn't come to terms with what he'd just heard, before he suddenly flew off the handle.

"Wh-What are you saying?! Why not?!"

"I already told you why, didn't I?" Kaoru answered coolly, "Over and over again at that! You're causing trouble for the other customers, and I've had enough. Someone else will be in charge of taking your orders from now on, and I won't be taking any more of your requests for counseling, either."

Fernand's legs almost gave out when Kaoru glared at him. Granted, most normal people would tremble in fear if Kaoru truly put everything into glaring at them, especially since she already had that harsh look in her eyes to begin with.

"B-But I'm a paying customer! You can't do that to a—"

"The manager told me he'd be fine without your business if you tried getting involved with me any further."

The other customers murmured their surprise that even the owner of the restaurant had gone this far.

"Wh-What... What are you..."

The only ones who had ever told Fernand "no" were his parents and his two friends. A bubbling anger built up inside him at being denied, until it swallowed him completely.

He suddenly grabbed her arm and yanked her toward him. "Come with me!"

"Ow! Stop it!"

Fernand was trying to drag Kaoru away from the restaurant as she struggled against him.

"A girl like you doesn't belong here. You're coming back with me!"

Aimee and Agathe came running over to stand in front of him, and the other customers got up as well to block his path. The owner and the chefs also came sprinting out of the kitchen with the same goal in mind.

"Get out of the way! Do you have any idea who I…"

He stopped halfway through his sentence, suddenly coming to terms with the cold stares fixed solely on him. That, combined with the look of disgust in Kaoru's eyes, caused him to lose the ability to speak. His head rapidly cooled off, and regret began building up inside him.

What was I doing here? Was I really about to let slip the fact that I'm royalty?

Fernand let go of Kaoru's arm, then silently left the restaurant.

"I'm sorry for causing so much trouble, everyone…"

Kaoru looked absolutely crestfallen as she apologized, but the customers around her immediately tried cheering her up, telling her, "It's not your fault at all, Kaoru!" and "We'll be here to protect you anytime you need it, so don't worry 'bout it!"

"A mug of ale on the house to everyone who stood up to protect Kaoru!" Cheers erupted inside the restaurant at the owner's words, since every single customer there had stood up for her.

It'd been three weeks since that incident. I hadn't seen Fernie back at the restaurant since then, and I spent my days in relative peace. Everyone at my workplace and all the customers had been really good to me, and I took a day off every ten days to go to the library to study up on where I was. Thanks to that, I'd gotten a pretty good grasp on everything I needed to know about this world—or this continent, I should say. I knew everything about the countries around me, and even their political climates.

Just like what Charles had told me back when I was hitching a ride with him and his dad, the Kingdom of Brancott was located at the base of a peninsula that stuck out to the west. The country was surrounded by oceans to the north and south, and by four other countries to the west and east. The political situation here was relatively stable compared to the other countries and, along with the Kingdom of Balmore to the north, Brancott was said to be a country that was very easy to live in. I'd say Celes ended up dropping me off in a pretty good place, considering it was her.

As I was thinking all this over while sweeping around the entrance to the shop, a super fancy carriage came up and parked itself right in front of the restaurant.

"You. Girl. Would this be the 'Big Belly Bistro'?" An arrogant-sounding voice called out to me from the open window of the coach.

That's right, I almost forgot how generic-sounding this place's name is...

"Oh, yes, it is."

Even if I wanted to snub him, nothing good would come of going against a noble—but I'd still go against them if I needed to, of course.

"Then would a girl by the name of 'Kaoru' be here?"

"Y-Yes, that would be me…"

Sirens were blaring in my head, telling me that nothing about this was good.

"What?!" With a shout, the man speaking stuck his face out the window. "You're telling me that Kaoru is this *little girl*?!"

Well excuuuse me for being little!

Everything about the haughty, chubby man practically screamed "aristocrat." He looked me up and down for a few seconds before sticking something that looked like a letter out the window of the coach. *Don't be so lazy about it, man…*

"Take it."

I didn't say a word as I reached out and grabbed the letter from him. I couldn't really just ignore him at this point, after all.

At the same time, someone stepped down from the other side of the coach and placed a decently sized trunk down on the side of the road. The window to the carriage closed, and the person who had set the box down got back in before the cart trundled away, without anyone explaining a thing to me.

"…The heck is this?"

I didn't know what it was, but I did know I had a bad feeling about it. And, somehow, I didn't think I was going to be wrong about that…

I hadn't touched the box at all, by the way. I mean, the guy hadn't said anything to me about it, and he'd left it in front of the hardware store right by us instead of the restaurant. That was probably a delivery for someone else, that's all. I'd just be a thief if

I tried touching it, so touch I shan't. No one said anything to me about it, and it was even delivered to a completely different place, so it didn't have anything to do with me. Nope, nothing at all.

After going back into the shop, I waited a little bit before checking again, only to find that the box was already gone.

Yup, looks like whoever that was supposed to be delivered to picked up their stuff. All right, let's move on to the problem at hand: the letter.

I opened the envelope with great trepidation, and inside I found a single sheet of paper. It was an invitation to a party being held at the royal palace next week.

All right, looks like my hunch was right on the money!

…I wasn't happy about that at all, though.

Viscount Alemann wasn't in a good mood. He'd been entrusted with delivering an invitation for the party being held next week by the prince, which was a good thing. This wasn't an invitation that had been made en masse to be sent to the other party guests, but something given to him directly from the prince. This was something to be ecstatic about. The recipient was probably someone the prince's heart was set on. He'd thought there must be some good fortune waiting for him at being made the bearer of such happy news…but the moment he thought that, he made the woeful discovery that the invitation was addressed to a commoner!

The prince is using me, a viscount, *as an errand boy for some commoner!*

He almost fainted from the humiliation. Not only was he being made to deliver this commoner's invitation, but a trunk with a dress, shoes, and a handwritten letter from the prince himself. Was this girl his secret lover or something? Was he planning on revealing her in front of everyone at the party? He may be able to use that information to his advantage…

…is what Alemann thought, but it turned out the recipient was just a child. She did have good features, but the look in her eyes was awful; "make other children cry" awful. There was no feasible way she could be his lover. All Alemann could wonder was what sort of cruel joke this was…

He had a duty to deliver the prince's letter personally, so he made sure to hold the farthest corner of the invitation as he handed it through the window of his coach, so that he wouldn't have to risk being touched by a commoner. There was no need for him to hand over the box with the dress and shoes in it himself, so he made the attendant with him set it down. After finishing his unpleasant task, he immediately left for home.

Oh, what a truly horrible day this was…

Doesn't look like I can wiggle my way out of this one, huh…

I'd ignored that box from earlier on purpose, and it wasn't like I didn't have my hunches over what that invitation could be about. It was true I wanted someone here who would support me—but not like this.

I already had tons of food packed away in my Item Box, as well as all the money I'd saved up from my job. I had learned my lesson from last time and made sure to stock up on plenty of water, too. Potions just didn't do the trick when it came to washing your face… or that's the feeling I got, at least.

All right then. Time to prepare myself for the worst.

Six days later, I had the manager and all my co-workers gather together, after telling them I had something important to talk about. I came clean and told them how some higher-up had singled me out and summoned me to appear tomorrow. I didn't tell them about how they had called me to the palace or anything, but I figured I should at least give them a heads-up so it didn't come back to bite me later. Everyone was shocked, and even recommended I run away right now if I didn't like it, but I laughed it off and told them I would be fine. Aimee and Agathe were crying and clinging to me, but that was probably because they'd be losing their other source of income, right? *Sorry about that, girls...* Everyone else there was sad over me leaving as well.

The past few months had been relatively peaceful, and I'd managed to get a grasp on this country's culture, economy, and almost everything else you could want to know. Now would've been just the right time for me to look for a place to begin settling down... if this hadn't happened. This town could've been where I started my new life proper, but it didn't look like that was going to happen anymore.

I would work lunchtime as normal tomorrow, then leave the restaurant for good right after. I couldn't just run away now. I was going to the palace, just watch. I'd make sure to put an end to this, and in a way where they weren't going to send people chasing after me again.

The time was evening, and the place was the main entrance to the castle.

"Excuse me..." a single noble girl called out to the guard standing at the gate, "I received an invitation for the party, so may I go through?"

The guard was taken aback by her words. He knew there was a party being held today, and he knew of the droves of nobles who were invited as well. But if she was supposed to be nobility, normally she should have arrived with the rest of her family in a carriage bearing their family crest. At the very least, a noble's daughter would never come walking up to a party. Ever.

Though it was obvious she didn't exactly look like the type of person to be invited to a party at the palace, she was wearing a dress no commoner would be able to get their hands on. Most importantly of all, she had an invitation. If he were to turn away the daughter of an aristocrat who was actually invited, heads would roll—more specifically, his head. And that wasn't a figure of speech.

Those eyes… They were the eyes of someone who was used to tormenting those below her! She had to be the wicked daughter of some aristocrat's family, no doubt about it! This wasn't a girl to be trifled with!

The girl gave the guard a slight bow before heading through the gate.

Kaoru slipped in with the other guests pouring into the castle, wandering around to find a room to be in. She finally found herself a dressing room, filled with older and younger women alike, fixing their dresses, tightening their corsages, redoing their makeup—it was pretty much an all-purpose room for girls here. She took off her "hand-me-down" from the baron's daughter, which she'd snuck off with during her escape a while back, before changing into her maid outfit (also taken from the baron's mansion). Who would have thought the daughter's old clothes would come in handy so often?

After she finished changing, Kaoru quietly left the room before finding an older maid with an air of dignity about her.

"Um, excuse me. I was told to head where the party is…"

The woman turned around, looking Kaoru over with bloodshot eyes. "Great, some backup from one of the other noble families! Do you have any experience serving drinks? Do you think you can hold about five or six glasses on a tray and walk around the room?"

Though Kaoru couldn't help but notice how scary the woman's eyes were, she decided she wasn't exactly one to talk.

"Y-Yes, I've had some experience as a waitress…"

"All right, then you'll be a great help! Go into that room over there and find some clothes you can change into! After that, head out to the party and circle around out there! If the supervisor out on the floor tells you anything different, follow their directions instead. Now hurry!"

"A-All right!"

Swept along at the woman's urging, Kaoru dashed off to get changed.

Prince Fernand had a sour look on his face as he scanned the venue of the party. It was around then that Allan came over to talk with him, finally back from home and wearing some clothes an actual noble would wear, for once.

"What's with the scary face, Fernie? I heard this party was supposed to be some informal way for you to choose who you'd be getting hitched to, but none of the ladies are going to come close if you look like that."

Allan probably hadn't gone back to the restaurant since he'd come back, since he didn't bring up the incident with Fernand and Kaoru.

"I was just looking for someone, is all."

"Hmm… Looking for someone, huh…"

An endless parade of aristocrats and potential bachelorettes had already come to visit with the prince, so there was no need for Fernand to look for anyone. Allan was well aware of this, which was why he looked a bit confused about what he had just heard.

"Fernand, none of your potential marriage candidates are going to come near you if you keep that look on your face."

"You too? Really?"

As Fabio showed up to make that comment, it was fairly obvious that Fernand was fed up over hearing the same thing again. But Fabio's next words, however, caused his eyes to fly wide open.

"By the way, I just saw that Kaoru girl not too long ago. I wonder why she's here… She looked quite busy, so I didn't have the chance to ask her myself."

"What?! Where, where did you see her?!"

Fabio and Allan were a bit taken aback when faced with Fernand's sudden change in attitude.

"Well, uh…she was just over there a moment ago…"

Fernand dashed off immediately in the direction Fabio pointed, his two friends hurrying to follow after him.

"Hey! What's up with you all of a sudden?!"

Allan and Fabio were thrown for a loop at seeing Fernand do a complete about-face, after he'd mostly sulked around until now.

"Hm? Oh, I thought she'd just ignored my invitation, but it looks like she's here after all."

"An invitation?" Fabio looked confused upon hearing those words. "But she wasn't exactly—"

When Fernand finally spotted Kaoru, he ended up yelling in shock. "Wh-Why are you wearing that outfit?! And why are you working as a server out here?!"

133

"Well, I'm a waitress…and I'm a waitress. Don't you think it'd be normal for me to wear this?" Kaoru answered coolly. But on the inside…

So it was him behind this, after all…

A silence fell over the room at the commoner girl's disrespectful attitude toward the prince.

"I'm not talking about that! I'm asking why a guest I invited here is *working* as a maid!"

A guest???

The nobles around them were all in silent shock at those words.

"I mean, I'm just a commoner girl working as a waitress. If someone told me to come to a party at the castle without any explanation whatsoever, don't you think I'd assume it was to help out the wait staff? There's no way I could be a guest. I don't even have a dress for these things," Kaoru answered indifferently.

"Wh-What…?!" Fernand went speechless for a moment, then yelled out across the room, "Viscount Alemann! Where is Viscount Alemann?!"

"Y-Yes, right here!" Alemann came running through the crowd after his name was called.

Fernand fixed the man with a glare. "Viscount Alemann, I specifically made a request to you, did I not? Deliver her the invitation, the dress, the shoes, and my letter. How do you explain this?!"

"I-I certainly delivered them to her!" the viscount stammered, sweating bullets.

"You say that, but look at her!"

"Oh, is this the person who came to the restaurant? All he said back then was 'take this' and handed me the invitation to the castle before leaving," Kaoru answered Fernand's question for Alemann.

"What about the dress and the letter?!"

"I haven't the faintest idea..."

"That is not true!" The viscount turned white as a sheet when he heard their conversation. "I delivered that box with the dress, shoes, and your letter in it!"

"Box? Are you talking about the package delivered to the place next door?"

"...What?"

"Well, another person came out of the carriage and left a box or something near the shop next to ours..."

"Wh-What happened to that package?!" Fernand shouted furiously.

"He didn't say anything about it, so I wasn't going to take a package that I thought was for the store next door. When I checked in on it a little while after, the box was already gone. I thought whoever it was for took it away."

"Then the dress...and my letter..." Fernand shot a menacing glare at Alemann. "What is the meaning of this? We'll be discussing this in detail later, Viscount Alemann."

It seemed like the growl in Fernand's voice was coming from the depths of hell itself. All color had drained from the viscount's face, and he began quivering.

"But that doesn't matter now!" Fernand one-sidedly continued the conversation. "Though you may be here because of a misunderstanding, what matters is that you're here. This is nothing to worry about. Now, come here! I'll introduce you to everyone as my wife-to-be."

"Whaaaaaat?!"

The nobles, Allan, Fabio, and Kaoru herself all let out a cry of shock.

"Wh-What in the world do you think you're saying?!" I shook off Prince Fernand's hand as he tried dragging me up onto the stage. "There's no way a commoner could do that!"

"There's no problem if we just have you become the adopted daughter of some earl's household."

"You have the order of this all wrong!" I fired off a rebuttal at the prince's words, "I should have been adopted *before* you asked to marry me! Even then, you would have to make sure to not let anyone pry into my past or where I came from, but no one's going to believe that after I've already announced to *everyone* that I'm just a commoner! Not only a commoner, but a waitress at that! I would just be made fun of behind my back, and none of the aristocrats from other countries would even *think* about talking with me!"

Prince Fernand sent another bitter glare at Viscount Alemann.

"And then, there's still the most important issue of all!" I declared, pointing my finger at him, "Did you actually check to see if I even *wanted* to marry you?"

His only response was a blank expression on his face. It was the type of face that said he never expected me to reject him once I knew he was a prince.

"The answer is no! I absolutely refuse!"

"*WHAAAAAAAAAAT?!*"

"Being a princess is on my top-three list of jobs I'd never *ever* want to do! You have no privacy, you can't get close to the people you want to, you have to fake a smile and talk to people you don't like, your children get taken from you by your wet nurse and you never get the chance to be a real family with them, and you have to go to parties all the time with other nobles or royal families from other countries! That's not to mention that you're pushing out babies until you get a boy, and if you get a girl you have to marry her off for diplomacy later! Your husband will even go off and have children with other women like it's no big deal! *Nothing* about that life sounds fun to me!"

One of the queens who'd come over to see what the fuss was about just stiffened up… *Ah, now she's crying.*

"It's pretty much the same thing with counts and earls and all that. You're barely allowed to leave the house, and outside of the odd party, the only people you end up talking to are your servants. Even then, the difference in status is so big that it's not like you're going to be friends with them. In fact, they would never dare speak their own opinion to you, and would instead just follow your orders to the letter. Your husband would always be gone because of work, and you'd have your in-laws always breathing down your neck for a successor to their household. Then they'll pester you about how you have to follow the traditions of the family you married into, and tell you how you're a member of *their* family now, so there's no need for you to go back home, and that their grandchildren only belong to them, and so on and so forth. Let's not forget how your husband can use the excuse that they need many, many children to cheat on you like there's no tomorrow, and you could end up stuck living in the same house as the woman he's cheating on you with and *their* children as well."

Several other wives crumpled to the ground in tears. An older noble grabbed the man who looked to be the husband of one of the wives. I wondered if that was the wife's father…

"That's why a viscount or a baron would be nice. They're still nobles, but are a bit more far-removed from the power struggles you would find elsewhere. You can also be a little closer to the help because of your position, like having tea together and chatting with them. You can even raise your own children along with the wet nurse or maids that babysit them. When your son gets a little bigger, you can travel around your territory with him, having the people celebrate your child on their birthday or things like that. It seems like you would have a much happier life spending time with your family and the people living in your domain."

The girls who had their eyes on some of the higher-ranking nobles looked around nervously. While it was true their parents wanted them to marry someone of high rank, the parents didn't want to make the daughters unhappy. At the same time, it was plain to see several upper-class nobles wincing. Probably the parents and step-parents of sons waiting to get married and carry on the family lineage.

"That's why the only way I'd want to marry into money is if I could find the rich son of a merchant, or even a lower-ranking noble. I would never want to be with someone who is of higher rank at the cost of a boring or stressful life. I'll leave that to the *actual* daughters born into nobility, the ones who live lives of luxury because they've sucked the people dry with taxes, or who are ready to give everything for their country in exchange for having a higher education."

Silence fell over the party.

"I don't care about any of that!" Fernand cried out, "I want you, and your knowledge! With your beauty and wisdom, I want you to help me develop this country even more! Together!"

"Knowledge? Beauty and wisdom? Those are all just things you want to use for yourself, aren't they? So it's not that you actually love me, you just want to *use* me. Then what about me, huh? Do you not care about what I feel? Is that something you don't have to take into consideration just because you're a prince?"

"W-Well…" The words caught in the prince's throat, making him unable to answer me.

I picked up a plate from a nearby table and slammed it against the table. A noise accompanied the shattering of the tableware, and I stooped down to pick up one of the fragments of the broken plate. All eyes were on me as the guests wondered what in the world I was doing.

Shng!

I used the plate shard to slash open my right cheek.

"Wh-Wh-What are you doing?!"

Blood dripped down from my face. The women let out screams, while Fernand was rendered speechless. The other nobles could only stand there, dumbfounded.

"There, now I'm nothing more than a foolish and unsightly girl. I'm worth nothing to a prince like you; just a commoner with nothing to offer. Now you should have no more business with me, right?"

After I finished saying my piece, no one even tried stopping me as I walked out of the party.

The guests at the party began stirring once more, and the first words to break the silence were finally spoken:

"What rash remarks! What disrespect—"

"What elegance!" one of the counts present shouted over the voice seeking to condemn Kaoru, "She knew the prince marrying a commoner such as herself would only disrupt the political balance here, so not only did she give up on being queen, she even went so far as to sully her own beautiful visage! And she used all that coarse language to make herself look like the villain here... Though she may just be a commoner, she chose the peace of the country over the fear of being punished! What loyalty! What devotion!"

It may have seemed like a stretch, but those gathered there had no choice but to accept it as fact to preserve the prince's dignity. No one would complain as long as it meant that the commoner girl would be kept safe behind the pretense. Besides, if Prince Fernand's reputation had suffered too much, that would bolster the people who were backing Prince Ghislain, the second prince, instead. If the girl had gone so far as to injure herself to protect Fernand, then no one would be able to say anything contemptuous about the prince, for fear of turning her efforts to naught.

This sudden declaration was quick thinking on the part of one of the earls backing Fernand, and the partygoers were all caught up in the moment. There were voices of admiration coming from all over the venue, signaling that the earl's plan had gone off well.

"Fernand, my friend... What did you *do*?" Allan looked down on Fernand with scorn as the prince knelt on the ground.

"I had just made the necessary arrangements with my father to look into her background, so we could be ready to bring her here at any time..." The disappointment in Fabio's voice was evident.

"Life actually might have been pretty fun if she ended up being your fiancée…"

Fernand lamented the foolishness of what he'd done when he heard Allan's words. But a broken plate was never going to be the same as it was before.

"Allan and I will go to the restaurant tomorrow *by ourselves* to see her. Please don't come with us. I'll see if we can't get some money together for her, or maybe a way to get her another job, since I'd imagine she won't be able to work at the restaurant anymore…"

Fernand barely managed to whisper a "please do" in response.

Ow, ow, ow, ow, ow!!!

The moment I left the party, I whipped up a painkiller-and-styptic combo potion and drank it all at once. The pain from the gash on my cheek calmed down right away.

All right, no one's following me. Time to make my escape from the capital!

I headed straight for the city gates. People were looking at me in shock as I jogged through the streets at night. An eleven- to twelve-year-old girl, wearing a first-class maid outfit from the royal palace, with her face smeared with blood, who also had a harsh look in her eyes… Yeah, anyone would be a little surprised by that.

I finally made it to the gates and called out to the guard there.

"Pardon me, but I need to leave!"

The gates leading out of the capital closed once nighttime fell, and would only be opened for the odd passerby coming in and out of the city. It was around this time a small girl called out, asking permission to leave. The kind-hearted guard took his lamp and left his station to see what all the fuss was about. Depending on what her story was, he was planning on detaining her and convincing her not to leave. It was dangerous outside the city walls at night.

"What happ— Whoa!" The guard let out a shout once he saw Kaoru's face smeared with blood.

"I got on the wrong side of some nobles, and I have to leave town right away…"

Though the gash on her cheek had stopped bleeding, it still left an awful scar. It may have healed cleanly if it were just a straight cut, but injuries like this where the flesh was rent completely were bound to leave a scar. Though she was still young, this was a blemish that would affect her for the rest of her life. If she was running away from nobles, who could lash out at her for any reason at any time, it might actually be safer outside the city walls.

"Wait just a second."

The guard had given up trying to detain Kaoru, heading inside his barracks for a second before returning and handing something to her without a word. It was a leather pouch with water inside, something that looked like dinner, and five silver coins.

"Um, what's this…?"

"Take it with you."

The guard quickly opened the small gate for her. Bowing her head to the guard, Kaoru hurried through the open doors.

After walking for a short while, she created a health potion and drank it down. The cut on Kaoru's face healed completely before fading away.

"Oops, I kept the maid outfit I got from the castle… Oh well. This may come in handy down the line!"

All she had to do to get rid of the bloodstains was make some type of cleansing potion.

Her next stop was the capital of the Kingdom of Balmore: Grua.

"All right, let's get going!"

Several years later—

A lone city guard was hurrying on his way home, looking worse for wear.

The man's son had been badly injured in a horrible accident last year. Though it was a miracle that he didn't lose his life, the young boy had lost his sight in his right eye, and he could barely see out of his left. At this rate, it was only a matter of time before he wouldn't be able to see out of that eye, either...

Of course the man felt heavy-hearted for his son when he thought about his future. If only he had those "tears of the goddess" he'd heard rumors of... It was a legendary medicine, said to be yellow in color, and found within an elegant glass bottle. But it was said to be something that even the nobles had trouble getting their hands on, so it was out of reach for a simple commoner like himself.

"Welcome home, dear. A little girl was here earlier, and she brought something addressed to you."

After his wife greeted him, the man went over and opened up the small box she'd left on the table. Inside were several assorted items, as well as a letter.

Who could this be from? And just what *is it, anyways...*

As he began reading over the letter, an expression of shock eventually took over his face. He grabbed something from the box before shouting out for his son.

"Joshua! Joshua!"

His son gingerly approached him, surprised to hear the unusual fervor in the man's voice. He took the bottle filled with medicine and had Joshua drink it. The next moment...

"Huh? I... I can see? And there's no scars either... Why?"

The man held his son tight and cried, while his wife ran over in shock.

On top of the table was the same box, filled with just a few things—and a letter.

"Thank you for everything you did for me. I'm returning the things I borrowed from you back then. As thanks, I've included something called the 'tears of the goddess' as well."

Also in the box was a familiar leather pouch and five silver coins.

The man had been promoted from his job as gatekeeper to being a city guard, but he still remembered the young girl he had lent a helping hand to all that time ago.

The tears wouldn't stop flowing.

"Goddess…"

Chapter 6:
Laying Low

It'd been a few days since I had begun my trip to the neighboring country's capital. Luckily for me, I happened to get a lift from another kind merchant. It was times like these where it was really useful that I looked way younger than fifteen. Oh, hey, maybe I'd even be able to stretch out my time looking to get hitched at this rate.

That gatekeeper guy was really nice, though. To be honest, I already had plenty of water and food in my Item Box, but it was so sweet of him to be worried about me that I just took it without saying anything. I'd have to make sure to thank him somehow, when I got the chance.

The merchant I was riding with said he happened to own a shop in the capital, but he'd occasionally leave and do business on his own to gather more information, as well as to not forget the basics of his trade. Yep, that was pretty much what every merchant should aspire to. It seemed like the guy would leave his son in charge of the shop while he was gone, but that same son told him to stop going on these trips because of how dangerous it was for him.

I was bored, so I'd moved up to sit next to the merchant so I could chat with him. He was a resident of Grua, the capital of Balmore, so I definitely should get something useful out of talking to him. Grua was on my list of places I might want to settle down, so I had to find out all I could about it.

"Oho, so that store's sales actually *dropped*, you say?"

"That's right. People weren't seeing the prices as half-off on the weekdays; rather, the prices were double on days off. They called the normal prices a rip-off, since they figured that store was able to make a profit selling things at half-price anyway."

"I see…"

The merchant was pretty interested in my story about a certain fast food restaurant that went under in my past life (I guess that's what you'd call it?) in Japan, so we worked out a deal where I would tell him more business horror stories from back home, in lieu of paying for the ride.

"So even though the store was trying to get rid of their leftover food by offering huge discounts on it all right before closing, all their customers would just wait for the discounts without actually buying anything."

"Hmm… So it's just like I thought."

Oh, has our merchant friend thought about giving discounts right before closing shop for the day? Then maybe I'll tell him about this next…

"I see… So since they offered that sort of service, it made those deal-seeking customers, who they couldn't make a profit off of, stay longer, while the regular customers had no place to sit and left… Goodness, the service business is hard to figure out."

Alrighty, let's try talking about marketing next…

"Featured bargain items you use to draw customers in? Package deals?! That's just an affront to the trade business itself!"

Well how 'bout that, he's an honest-to-God businessman after all. I guess I'll tell him about some more ethical business techniques then.

"Customer loyalty, you say? And you narrow down the type of customer you want? But if you do that, then won't you end up losing a portion of your customers instead...? Wait, don't aim for one out of a hundred, but for two out of ten? Tell me more about how that works!"

...Why is he *the one asking* me *for more information here?!*

She's a pretty interesting gal.

The Abili Trade Company was said to be one of the most prominent enterprises you could find in the royal capital—and it also happened to be *my* company.

I'd worked my way up from when I was just peddling wares out of my one wagon, but found myself in a bit of a rut as of late. I began longing for the days where I had no money but had enjoyed getting out there and selling things, so I left my store to my son and went out on a bit of a trading journey. I was almost back to Grua when I happened to pick up a young girl along the way. She looked to be about eleven or twelve, and was strolling with barely any luggage to be seen. She said she was on her way to the capital as well, but where could she have been walking from while carrying almost nothing on her? Judging by the way she walked, it would take her much longer to get where she was going compared to any normal person. She had such a delicate-looking body that it wouldn't even take a monster to finish her off... Maybe a single stray dog would be enough to spell the end for her. I had a daughter as well, so I couldn't just leave her be.

There was space in the back of my wagon, but she seemed a bit bored, which was probably why she came and joined me up in the passenger seat. She asked me a whole slew of questions about the capital, and it sounded like she was looking for work there. The conversation eventually turned to the trading business, and she started telling stories about "stores she knew" or "what she heard from other people." I was shocked, frankly. How did she know so much? No merchant worth their salt would tell some girl living out in the sticks these sorts of things so easily. She wasn't just repeating these stories without understanding what they meant either—she understood why these things happened, and was even adding her own opinions on the stories. Not only that, but she had some pretty sharp takes on them too!

I hadn't really thought about discounting things until now. It cost money to get inventory for the store, and you had to find a way to make reasonable profits off it all despite that. You also had to consider the trust between the maker, vendor, and buyer, as well. You couldn't sell your products at too high or low a price; you had to find an appropriate cost for it. Any merchant should want to avoid doing anything to disrupt the flow of the marketplace. But what this girl told me about pricing and discounts had really captured my interest. There were things that reaffirmed my convictions about the trade business, and she also offered some very appealing ideas, as well. She kept saying she'd only heard these stories from someone else, but it was obvious there was some other reason behind why she knew all this. This was a girl for whom I could look forward to seeing what the future had in store.

If she's looking for a job, then she should have no qualms about coming to work for me. I'm sure she'd happily accept as soon as she heard the name of my company. All right, that's what I'll do!

The wagon arrived at the gates to the capital. It would only be a few minutes until the two reached the end of the line to get inside.

"If you want, how about coming to work for me, Kaoru? The job comes with a place to stay as well, so you don't have to worry about finding living arrangements."

The girl thought it over for a second, before smiling and giving her answer.

"Thank you, but it's all right. I'll look for work on my own."

"Huh? Oh, right, I haven't said the name of my company yet! I may have been out on a trip for my own fun, but I'm actually the owner of the Abili Trade Company. That's right: I'm *the* Johann Abili, head of Abili Trade!" he declared confidently, a big grin on his face, "Well? Surprised?"

"...I see. Oh, I have to register as a newcomer, so I guess this is where we part ways. Thank you very much for letting me ride with you. I enjoyed talking with you as well. Until we meet again!"

The girl hopped down from the wagon and walked away. Johann Abili, the head of the Abili Trade Company, could only watch in blank amazement as she did so.

"Um... The Abili Trade Company is said to be one of the most prominent enterprises in the capital, and is even famous in other countries, with tons of people who would love to work there... It's the one place anyone from the countryside would love to get in with... You know, *that*...Abili...Trade Company..."

Johann's voice gradually became weaker and weaker, before petering out entirely.

That merchant seemed like a pretty nice guy with a large shop, but working at a place like that means I'd have to start from the bottom. I'd probably just be loaded down with a whole bunch of busywork as a newbie, too. Pretty sure I'd have tons of coworkers and people working above me, so there's a good chance I wouldn't even get any time to myself. Seems doubtful I'd have any days off, either. I don't want to keep doing menial labor my whole life here. I need to be out there gathering information and getting things in order so I can open my own shop someday, so I want to find a job that lets me be a little more flexible with my free time. Once I've done enough prep work, I need to start making a name for myself, and all sorts of other stuff to get my shop ready, too.

No matter how big and famous the shop may have been, if it didn't match up with Kaoru's goals, then there was nothing else to be said on the matter.

I'd made my way to the job-hunting agency in Grua.

Hmm, I wonder if there are any good ones here... I pondered to myself as I browsed through the available jobs.

A good while had passed since I began looking at the postings. I'd already gone to the receptionist to apply for two of them that would've been perfect, but she turned me down because she thought I was a minor. They weren't even anything fishy, either...

There was a man doing office work here who saw me get rejected, and called out to the receptionist.

"Hey, Aria, how about recommending her that one job at Bardot's place?"

"Oh, that one? Let's see..."

The receptionist looked me over for a few seconds before calling out to me.

"How are you with housework, miss? Cooking, cleaning, those sorts of things."

Mom and Dad both had full-time jobs, so I'd been doing chores and taking care of the house since I was in middle school. Just leave it to me!

"My mother was always working, so I'm great at housework and taking care of kids!"

"Great, then this might work out after all. I have a housekeeping job that comes with a place to stay, as well. What do you say?"

According to the receptionist, there was a small workshop that had put out a help-wanted ad for someone to basically come and work as a maid for them. Including the owner, there were five of them working there in total, and it was supposed to be a bit of a…"quirky" workshop. They weren't bad people by any means, but none of the help they took on seemed to stick around for long. They would often come back to repost their ad, and the amount they paid in fees to the agency was nothing to sneeze at.

For the job itself, they needed someone who could cook, clean, do laundry, and do other odd jobs around the workshop. Everyone besides the owner himself commuted there, but they would all eat at the workshop together, probably because it was too much trouble for them to go all the way home to make food for themselves.

It wasn't supposed to be a job that kept you busy around the clock, and it sounded like I was free to do whatever I wanted, so long as I finished the work they asked me to do. I could go out and about during the day if I was done cooking, for example. They even gave the help days off too. It seemed like the workers would go out to eat on those days, or make do with what they had on hand. It sounded like they'd gone through a few periods of not having anyone to help out, so I guess they had learned to do at least that much.

But wait, seriously? This is, like, the perfect job for me!

"A pleasure to meet you. My name is Kaoru; I was referred here by the job-hunting agency."

"Nice to meetcha. There's no need to be so stiff at our place, so feel free to relax and be yourself," the man said with a smile. He was Bardot, the current head of the Maillart Workshop, and I was incredibly happy to hear how lax he was with the formalities.

"Let's call these next few days a 'trial period,' if you don't mind. All those fees to the agency keep building up, since our new hires always quit right away, and they've even started letting us get extensions for paying them now," Bardot said with a bitter grin, "Now, let's get you introduced to everyone. Honestly, just let me know anytime if you think it's not gonna work out. I'm already used to it by now, so it won't bother me at all…"

"All right, I understand."

Man, just how low is his self-esteem now…?

With that, he led me to the main workshop, which looked more like some sort of laboratory if you asked me. Then, the moment he opened the door…

"…Eugh…"

It reeks in here…

It smelled like sweat, B.O., chemicals…and like something was rotting. Seriously, did something die in here?

Next I saw four men, two of them currently sprawled out on the floor. One of them was middle-aged, two were young men, and one was just a boy. Well, I say "boy," but I guess he'd be considered an adult here.

"Carlos, Alban, wake up. We've got a new potential helper who I need to introduce!"

The two of them jumped up at Bardot's words.

"Thank the Goddess!"

"Hold it, this is just a trial run, got that? A *trial* run!" Bardot fired back, emphasizing the last part.

Beginning with the oldest, there was Carlos at thirty-two years old, Achille at twenty-one, Alban at nineteen, and Brian at sixteen. Everyone here was doing their best to become a first-rate engineer, apparently.

According to what Bardot had told me, this wasn't just a workshop that made things to sell to cover living expenses. It was something more akin to a research and development lab for new gadgets and products. They weren't getting any financial support for their work, though, so they'd also make goods they could sell to cover their research costs and make enough money for their everyday lives. They were all skilled at what they did, so the quality of their products was actually pretty good. The only problem was that they were a group of inventors who only cared about research, not profits, and weren't suited to be merchants. As such, they basically had no money. And since they were a group of inventors, the concept of "working hours" didn't exist for them. They could get so wrapped up in their research that they wouldn't bathe or change clothes for days, would forget to eat and eventually collapse from hunger, and would even spend days on end in the lab. They never ran out of things to say when it came to their research, but were clueless on what was going on in the world.

Ah, I get it. I'm basically here to babysit the five of them.

I finally had an idea what my job really entailed.

After the introductions were finished, we moved right into Q-and-A time. A flurry of questions came from the guys, one after the other.

"Can you cook and clean and stuff?"

"I'm probably as good at cleaning as the next person, but I'm pretty confident in my cooking skills. I always cooked for my family, and the restaurant I worked at before this even decided to serve some of the dishes I'd made."

The expectation in their eyes was at an all-time high.

"So when you're cleaning, there are a few things we want you to be aware of…"

"Oh, like how everything looks messy, but you actually have it like that on purpose and know where everything is? Or that even things that look like scraps of paper actually have something really important written on them, so you don't want me to throw them away? Or like how there's plenty of dangerous chemicals here, so I shouldn't try to smell, touch, mix, or toss them?"

"Whoa…"

"Um… Have you ever worked in a place like this before?"

"No, not really."

"…"

"Erm, well… We lose track of time a lot when we get into our work, and sometimes we just forget to eat…"

"Aren't all boys like that?"

The four of them turned to look at Bardot, their eyes brimming with hope. Even Bardot looked somewhat cheerful about the whole thing. It was like they were all thinking I might be the one to actually stay.

Yup, I already know plenty *about how to handle boys, thanks to living with my dad and big brother.*

Several days later, I was officially hired for the job, and the workshop paid the job-hunting agency the fee for my referral.

I was knocking the cooking thing out of the park, if I did say so myself. I got better at recognizing the right time for when everyone was about to reach a good stopping point in their work, and at finding ways to get them fed, even if they all came in at different times. Eventually, I innovated (*cough cut corners cough*) and began making simple dishes like sandwiches and onigiri that they could eat while working on things in the lab, which made my job so much easier. I put my newfound free time to good use, doing things like walking around town and going to the library (going to the library was expensive in this country as well, so I didn't really go *that* often, though). And thanks to the "Kaoru's Special Deodorizer" I'd told them I made from fruit juice and tea and a bunch of other stuff, the horrible death-stench in the workspace became something actually tolerable.

Because of all that, I'd secured myself a place as an invaluable asset here in the workshop.

"Oh? Are you making something, Achille?"

One day, I'd spotted Achille working on something to sell to make a profit instead of his usual research, so I called out to him.

"Yeah, it's a flask. Kinda like a canteen or something that you can put alcohol or other strong spirits in. I'm supposed to make it lightweight and sturdy, and make it out of something that won't affect the taste of what you put in it. We should be able to sell the extra high-quality ones to aristocrats for a good price. That said, it's a whole other story trying to make ones from metal with fancy decorations and stuff on them. What I'm working on here should be fine for normal, everyday use."

Surprisingly enough, Achille was the only member of the workshop who was actually a noble. That said, he was only the third son of a viscount. He still had another older brother, should something happen to the oldest one, so there was an extremely low chance he'd succeed his father and take over the household. Because of that, and due to Achille's decidedly un-aristocratic love of research and experimentation, his father allowed him to do whatever he pleased. That wasn't to say he was being abandoned or ignored, though, but his father was allowing Achille the freedom to do whatever he wanted with his future. He got along well with his brothers, and loved his family as well.

A container, huh... Maybe it's about time for me to make a move.

"Oh, that's right. I happen to know someone who does glass work. They've never tried selling it, because they do it for fun, but they've always said they wanted to try selling something at least once. You think we could try leaving one of the containers they made on the workshop store shelf?"

The store shelf was where we'd leave our products for customers to see for themselves, or to display our workshop's prowess in creating new goods. All the products on display had a price tag to go with them, so everything was indeed for sale as well. Since the workshop usually only made things to order, there was still plenty of space on the shelf.

"Hmm... I think it'd be all right, but you should probably ask Bardot if it's okay."

"All right, got it. I'll go try asking him then."

And just like that, I got permission to go ahead with my plan. This was a request from the girl who always worked hard, made delicious food, and, above all else, actually stayed. Anyone at the workshop seemed happy to grant almost any request I had for them.

"It's…"

Bardot and the others were at a loss for words when they saw the glass container I'd made.

"It's so beautiful…"

"The design and the craftsmanship goes without saying, but just look at how clear that glass is… Look at how it sparkles! Just what *is* this?!"

The workshop members were in shock over the glass container that my "friend" had made. It was a perfume bottle made of sparkling crystal glass that boasted an asymmetrical design and ended with an extravagantly large stopper at the top. The stopper itself was made to look like a winged goddess sitting on the lip of the bottle, and it was hard to tell if the bottle or the lid should be the main focus… No, scratch that—the stopper was *definitely* the main attraction here.

Crystal glass is created by adding lead oxide to the raw materials, making it much more translucent and sparkly than your average glass. It's a bit of a misnomer to call glass "crystal" when it lacks a crystalline structure, but we'll let that slide since it's just the commercial name for the glass itself. Anyway, it sells for a much higher price than your average glass back on Earth, and it hasn't actually been used in this world yet. Normally, it's better to cut crystal glass instead of stretch it, since that's the best way to bring out the natural sparkle it contains. It's a fairly common practice not to do too much extra work, to preserve that sparkle—but this container was different. There were a plethora of finer details worked into the glass, with almost every inch of it having been cut in some way.

"Kaoru… D-Do you think we could meet the person who made this?"

"Oh, the family of the girl who made this is pretty strict, actually. It seems like she made this in secret, when she wasn't doing her chores around the house. Besides, she doesn't do too well around guys…"

"Sh-She did it…in her spare time…"

Ah… They're more bummed out about that than not being able to meet my fake friend…

"Um, I can ask her to make more for us."

Oh, they recovered fast!

In the end, we called off putting the bottle on the store shelf. We'd already seen the reaction it caused here in the workshop, and it'd be a problem if people thought all our products were made with this much detail and quality. That was why I'd decided to find a noble who might be interested in purchasing it, and had them buy it directly from me instead.

The results: I'd sold it for a whopping three gold coins. I paid six small gold coins to the workshop as a handling fee, which was about the price of a month's worth of groceries to cook for everyone here (not including the price of the firewood I needed as well).

Not only did I have the power to create any medicine with the exact effect I wanted it to have, I could create any *container* I wanted it to be in, too.

Even if I can't sell potions or use my modern-day knowledge, I can still make money!

And so, my peaceful days helping out at the workshop continued. I had plenty of money, thanks to the crystal glass I'd sell every once in a while, and I could go to the library anytime I wanted, now. My Item Box was packed full of supplies, so I could tackle any unforeseen circumstances that came my way. I had plenty of food, spare clothes, a knife, some flint, and even a warm blanket, to name just a few things. I was hoping nothing would happen, since I wasn't planning on running away from anything right now. This was all just in case, though.

I'd finally gotten to the point I could say I knew as much as the average person living here, so all that was left now was to find someone who had my back and to carve out a place for myself in the world. It wasn't like I hated how I was living right now, but I wasn't planning on being a housekeeper my entire life here, you know? I'd been reincarnated in a whole different world with cheat powers, so I wanted to have a bit more freedom with how I lived my life. The one and only Goddess of this place had even told me it was all right to influence the world if I wanted to. First, I would play it safe and make a plan for myself. After that, it probably wouldn't be a bad idea to be proactive and get myself some self-protection. It'd be nice if I could help people out with my potions somehow, as well.

I guessed there was no rush, though. For now, I'd just wait for my chance to come...

One day, when Kaoru was cleaning the entrance to the workshop, a street urchin happened to pass by her. When they were gone, they left a balled-up piece of paper in their wake. She stooped down to pick it up before sticking it in her pocket. She was cleaning after all, so it was only natural for her to pick up trash.

What wasn't natural, however, was what had just gone down.

No simple street urchin should have something as valuable as paper, and they certainly wouldn't just toss it away as garbage. Kaoru went to the kitchen before taking out the scrap of paper and reading what was written on it.

"a mother and a kid in the slums. shes honest she gives everything to raise daughter. nobles hurt her really bad, lashed out at her"

The note was written in an untidy scrawl by the only one of the vagabond children who could actually write.

Kaoru suddenly had plans for the evening.

After I made dinner and cleaned up after myself at the workshop, I made some late-night snacks for later and left them on the shelf before changing into some comfier clothes. Everyone was so focused on their work they didn't notice me quietly sneak outside. Even if they had, I was sure they'd let me off saying it was only a kid enjoying some nighttime fun.

After walking a bit, I saw a kid who looked to be a street urchin in front of me. I kept a good distance between us as I followed behind them. Eventually, I found myself with several other raggedy-looking kids trailing behind me. They kept their distance from me as well, keeping a wary eye on their surroundings. We walked along like this as we headed into the poor district of the city, eventually coming to a small shack of a house. The boy I was following stopped and gave me a signal, then went off to hide.

So this is the place…

I drank a potion to change the color of my eyes and hair, then put on a mask to hide my face, before donning a cloak and entering the shack.

"…Who is it?"

A little girl who couldn't be more than five or six was on full alert as she warily responded to me breaking and entering. The tone of her voice showed she was prepared to protect her mother, who was bedridden due to her injuries, at any cost. A person had just essentially broken into their house wearing a mask and a cloak… Yeah, even I couldn't think anyone else looked more suspicious than I did right now.

"Just a messenger," I answered the little girl in a gentle voice.

"...A messenger? From who?" the girl asked back, not letting down her guard.

"Celes."

"Celes? Who's that?"

"Oh, right. Maybe calling her 'Celestine' might make it easier to understand?"

"Ah!"

There was no blasphemer in this world who'd name their kid after the Goddess, and there wasn't anyone who would do evil in her name, either. She wasn't just an imaginary concept in this world, but had actually made appearances here up until a few decades ago. She was a real god who'd come down, save people, and hand down divine revelations.

"I want to give your mom some medicine. Would that be okay with you?"

"Yes, please!"

The mother was lying on the floor, staying so still I couldn't tell if she was sleeping or had lost consciousness. She looked to be in her late twenties, but I bet a native would say she looked about twenty-two or twenty-three. That was about the same age I was when I bit the big one back on Earth, and that was just when I'd gotten a job after graduating college. Here she was, working so hard to raise her kid, and she'd been beaten half to death just because an aristocrat was having a bad day?

Screw that! Like hell I'll just let that slide!

"The righteous shall be healed by my hands!"

I raised my right arm into the air and summoned forth a potion in the shape of a mayonnaise squeeze bottle, filled with a red potion. I had the little girl lift the upper half of the mother's body while I held open her mouth with my left hand, putting the tip of the bottle inside and gently wringing out its contents. The red liquid poured down her throat as the small girl gulped and watched me as I worked.

One one thousand, two one thousand, three one thousand, four one thousand...

Five one thousand, six one thousand, seven one thousand, eight one thousand...

"M...mmgh..."

"M-Mommy!"

"Ko...sha...?"

"Mommyyy!"

Right around the time Kosha stopped crying, the mother turned to look at me with a curious look on her face.

"U-Um... Who might you be?"

"Oh, I'm just a simple pharmacist. I'll be taking my leave now that we're all finished here. As for my fee..."

"What...?" Kosha and her mother both turned pale.

I already knew they didn't have money—but cash wasn't the only payment method I took.

"All right! Then you can pay me by letting me poke and squish Kosha's cheeks until I'm satisfied!"

"Huh?!"

"All done. Thanks for leading me here."

"Then we'll all be your escort on the way back to the workshop."

"Right, I'm counting on you."

"..."

Though he said that, Emile didn't budge an inch as he stared right at my face.

"Something the matter?"

"...Can I ask you something?"

"Sure, what's up?"

"Why does your face look so smooth?"

"...It's a secret!"

It had all happened a few weeks back. Kaoru was out in the marketplace doing some shopping when a street urchin had collided with her. She watched as the boy ran off without stopping before sticking her hand into her breast pocket.

Yup, it's gone all right...

It should go without saying, but she'd just been hit by a pickpocket.

Though she looked like a child herself, Kaoru would go out into the town market every day to buy groceries. Anyone who saw the armfuls of food she'd bring with her on the way back could guess she had a decent amount of cash on her. Since she was only a little girl, there was no need to worry about getting caught and taken away even if someone flubbed an attempt to steal from her. She was the perfect prey for street urchins and pickpockets. It was times like these when the Item Box came in handy. She kept her real purse stored safely away in there, while having a fake tucked away in her breast pocket. As for what was inside it, well...

Kaoru leisurely strolled in the direction the boy had run off in. Getting pickpocketed meant the perpetrator would take the cash out of the wallet once they were safe, then ditch the wallet itself. Even if there were people who wrote their name on it beforehand, no one would ever write it on their money; there wouldn't be any evidence left of the crime. That was why Kaoru had set up her fake wallet with something that happened almost instantly:

"AUUUGGGHHHHHH!"

There it is!

Kaoru followed the scream, finding herself face-to-face with a young boy clutching his right hand in agony. It was the same street urchin who'd bumped into her earlier. The boy's right hand had swollen, taking on a ghastly shade of purple. Apparently the pain was as bad as it looked—which is what she expected, since she'd made the potion to do just that. Tears welled up in the boy's eyes as soon as he saw Kaoru, pleading with her to help him.

Oh, fine...

Kaoru took a potion from her pocket and handed it to the boy, telling him to drink it. His hands shook as he downed the medicine, and the pain and swelling from his right hand were fixed almost immediately. She'd actually made it so the symptoms of her trap would disappear on their own after a few hours had passed, just in case the culprit managed to elude her. They'd have to suffer through the pain until that happened, though. Even if someone stole from her, it wasn't like she wanted to cause them any real harm. At most, Kaoru wanted to traumatize them a little with the experience.

"Stealing from a god, are we... You must not care much for your life, boy."

"Huh? G-God...?"

"You won't be getting off with just this when I bring down my next divine punishment," Kaoru said with a grin on her face.

"A-Ahhhhhh!"

The boy threw himself to the ground and prostrated himself before the girl as she placed her hands on her hips triumphantly. It was a very strange scene, the fiendish look in Kaoru's eyes just making it seem all the more suspicious. If she just stepped on the boy's head now, then…

…Wait, why did it turn out like this?

"I'd ask you what you're doing stealing…but I think I already know the answer."

It has to be so he can get himself something to eat.

"Actually, Belle hasn't been doing so good…"

Uh-oh, someone's sick… That changes things!

"Lead me there."

"H-Huh…?"

The boy had no choice but to comply, leading me to a run-down house in the slums with crumbling walls and a dilapidated roof. Living inside this ramshackle home were an assortment of seven boys and girls. I guessed they wouldn't really be street urchins if they actually had a place to live, huh?

When I asked who was sick here, they all raised their hands.

Got it, so that's how it is.

"Everyone, line up!"

All the kids looked especially confused when I said that, so I had the boy who had tried to pickpocket me earlier line them up for me since he seemed to be the oldest one of the group. Being eleven or twelve may be considered young here, but since I looked around fifteen or sixteen, tops, there shouldn't have been any problems with me putting him to work!

"All right, everyone come take turns getting one."

I handed out an assortment of potions to cure various injuries and diseases.

"All right, and here's another one."

Next, I whipped up a potion to restore their deteriorated muscles and organs, and even improve their health as well. It looked like they were all suffering from a variety of different afflictions, and I thought it might be a bit overboard trying to squeeze too many effects into one potion, which was why I'd split them up into two instead.

"Huh...?"

"My leg doesn't hurt?"

"I feel so light now!"

"My chest doesn't hurt anymore..."

The children let out cries of surprise one after the other.

Hmm... What to do, what to do...

At this rate, they'd just end up right back where they started. This was only a way to stave off the inevitable. But would some girl working as a housekeeper be able to look after all these kids? Should I have just ignored them in the first place since it had nothing to do with me? I thought not. I wouldn't have come here in the first place if I was going to do that.

I'd already said it myself, and I quote: "I wanted to have a bit more freedom with how I lived my life. The one and only Goddess of this place had even told me it was all right to influence the world if I wanted to. First, I would play it safe and make a plan for myself. After that, it probably wouldn't be a bad idea to be proactive and get myself some self-protection. It'd be nice if I could help people out with my potions somehow, as well." It was about time to do just that! Kaoru Nagase was the type of girl who avoided danger and always chose the safe way in life! (Though I did end up dead in some freak accident...)

So did that mean I was just going to repeat that same lifestyle again here? Was I just going to live my life protecting my close friends and family, even after I'd gotten these powers from the Goddess? Should I not get involved with other people?

That would be way too boring.

The old Kaoru Nagase was dead. I was a brand new Kaoru, given a fresh start in life here. I wasn't the same "Kaoru Nagase" from Japan, but just "Kaoru," a girl free to live her life the way she wanted in this world—and with permission from the Goddess who watched over this world, even!

"Listen up, kids!" I declared, placing both hands on my hips and sticking my chest out, "I'm Kaoru, a friend of the Goddess Celestine. She has given me free rein to do as I see fit and enjoy life in this world as a normal human."

Nothing I said was a lie so far, but the kids didn't really seem to get what I was talking about.

"Basically, she told me I can do whatever I want."

Nod, nod.

"That's why I want to offer blessings to those who are pure of heart, just like I did with you all."

The children finally came to realize, tears in their eyes, that it was a miracle that all their ailments had been cured. Even though their fellow humans had abandoned them and treated them like nothing more than garbage, they'd received the blessing of the goddess.

"However, trying to find those deserving of these blessings without being discovered by those who'd want to take advantage of them is quite the task, considering I've taken on the form of a human myself. That's where you all come in. How about becoming my assistants to help me out? As a reward, I'll keep you healthy, while bestowing you with all sorts of food."

The seven children all threw themselves down at my feet, and that was how I gained seven new members of my own personal defense force.

Afterwards, Kaoru had made sure to tell the children to keep this a secret. If someone appeared who wished to use the powers of the goddess for less than wholesome motives, then divine punishment would befall the world, and Kaoru would have to return to the heavens. Even if the kids tried to sell her out for money, a truly evil person wouldn't just pay for the information; they'd kill the children, so they'd be the only one who knew.

Though Kaoru would cure them and give the children enough food to get by, she claimed that just providing them with everything wouldn't make them successful people. She made sure to let them know that they'd have to work to earn anything other than that for themselves. The children had no reason to doubt her words, especially after having experienced her miracles with their own bodies. They turned away from crime and went for work running errands or other odd jobs to improve their quality of life. On top of that, they went around searching for rumors about purehearted souls suffering from injury or sickness, and served as the personal bodyguards to the goddess who'd come to the world as a human.

Kaoru had prepared herself a cloak and mask to hide her true identity. Though she was under the impression that it looked pretty cool, it was actually a little much. Like, enough to make a child cry if they ran into her in the middle of the night.

That was how Kaoru began working her miracles in secret. She used the information the children brought her to help those who needed it, one person at a time.

There was a rumor slowly spreading among certain people who lived in the capital:

Those who were righteous and pure of heart would receive the blessings of the goddess. You could never let anyone whose hearts were tainted by greed know of her existence, and you mustn't betray the goddess. The eyes of the goddess saw *everything*.

Back at the headquarters for the secret organization, "The Eyes of the Goddess"—

In reality, it was just a busted-up house, the same one the seven kids were living in.

"You really think we'll just stop there after being given such a cool name?"

"Never!"

They turned me down, even though I was supposed to be the goddess here...

Today I was extra lazy...er, ahem, very efficient...preparing meals for the workshop, so I thought I'd stretch my legs and head over to the slums to make dinner for the kids. They were always cooking for themselves, using a pot that had definitely seen better days, and the food they made was... I shouldn't sugarcoat it—it wasn't good. That's why I thought it was nice to do this every once in a while.

After dinner had wrapped up, they gave me their report. I'd already told the children how I was enjoying my life here, and they could just speak with me normally, as long as they kept my secret.

Basically, they could just think of me as a nice girl who would cook for them every so often.

"So that merchant's daughter is sick, then. But they must be pretty rich, right?"

"There are some things you can't fix with money. Besides, he's a really good person," insisted Emile, the leader of the ragtag group of kids, the one who'd tried pickpocketing me. Anyway, he made a good point. "This guy is always down here in the poor district offering food for everyone, but he always says the same thing: 'I'm nothing but a hypocrite. I only enjoy the self-satisfaction I get from this sort of charity work. I could get used to this feeling of superiority!'"

Oof... I mean, uh... They sound like a good person...I think?

It was the dark of the night when I knocked on the back door of a certain merchant's house.

"...Who is it?" a woman's voice answered in response.

"A thief, put 'em up! No, but seriously, it's the pharmacist."

"...Ah... Please, come inside."

It'd be impossible for an amateur like me to try sneaking my way into a big-name merchant's house, so I made sure they knew I was coming. That said, all I did was give some spare change to some random kid to deliver a letter to them beforehand. There was pretty much nothing more suspicious than that.

But as the doting parents of a sick daughter, they were grasping at straws looking for solutions, and I was supposed to be coming alone. Even if they were on high alert and had a guard or someone here, I figured they'd at least let me inside. If they knew their visitor was a child, I thought that'd make them a little less on guard...or it could have made them even more suspicious.

I had a backup plan in case they tried to catch me, of course: I'd already made an extra-strong batch of tear gas, which would cause a good deal of confusion and chaos. Since they didn't have any way of knowing what it was, they'd probably think a demon had suddenly appeared to wreak havoc or something. I'd drink something to neutralize the effects of the gas, then change my clothes and the color of my eyes and hair once I managed to get away.

"We heard you would be coming. Right this way, if you please."

The elderly servant who opened the door acted as my guide, leading me through the back garden and into the mansion, before showing me inside a room. She didn't even bat an eye at the sight of a little girl wearing a sketchy mask. She was a pro, no doubt about it... I guess I should've expected that from someone who worked for a big-name business.

The daughter in question was lying down in bed inside the room, her parents and brother sitting beside her in chairs. There were no guards to be seen. The jaws of the people inside dropped when they saw me enter the room. They were expecting the messenger of the goddess to be coming here, and they got a little girl wearing a weird mask instead. But could you really blame them for being a bit surprised?

"Wait, are you who I think you are?" I blurted out in surprise when I saw who was already sitting in the room. The person in front of me was the same guy who'd given me a lift all the way to the capital.

"Huh? Are you...Kaoru?"

Even after I'd gone out of my way to wear a mask and change the color of my eyes and hair, the merchant figured out who I was in an instant once he heard my voice.

"What are you doing here?" we said in sync.

"Wh-Why are you here, Kaoru?" the merchant asked, eyes wide open.

"Well, you know... I was just thinking of healing your daughter's illness, is all."

"Wait... D-Does that mean *you're* the messenger of the Goddess then?"

This was a guy who really understood the value of information. He'd already heard rumors of me, even though they shouldn't have spread this far yet.

"Yeah, something like that."

The merchant was at a loss for words, while his wife and son could only stare blankly.

Oh, whatever. I'm taking off the dumb mask. Wait...how come the lady who showed me inside just flinched when she saw my face? She looked like she couldn't have cared less when she saw me all incognito with my mask and cloak! Is it my eyes? Is the look I always have in my eyes really that *bad?! Well, I'm used to it by now, so it doesn't bother me* that *much... Yeah...*

"Have her drink this."

The merchant took the small bottle I offered him with trembling hands. Taking every care in the world not to spill it, he placed the bottle to his daughter's lips and had her drink what was inside. The pained expression on her face softened with each passing second, and the color returned to her cheeks. Her breathing calmed and soon steadied itself to a stable rhythm.

"Ohhh..."

The merchant, his wife, his son, and their servant all let out voices of admiration. Everyone here could see that the daughter had made a complete recovery.

"But why would the Goddess give her blessing to us?" the merchant asked me, his voice shaking.

"Well, you really helped me out back then. That, and I know all about how you feed people down in the poorer areas of town."

He'd been giving blessings in his own way to the downtrodden and unfortunate till now, but even the rich and powerful needed help sometimes. Some of them were even good people, too.

I was wary of the powerful, since I could only imagine them trying to use me for their less-than-wholesome motives. Still, I'd need to make myself some friends in high places if I wanted someone to have my back here. Thinking as much, it might be about time to go about looking for someone just like that…

"Ah… Ahhhhhh!" the merchant, Johann Abili, had broken down in tears.

Everything he'd done until now had come back to him as a way to save his daughter. Even though there were times he'd blasphemed against the Goddess, she'd still understood all the same. His faith and conviction had saved his daughter.

"Thank you for everything, dear angel…"

"Oh, no, please. You can just call me Kaoru, like you did before."

"But… Ah, I see… Yes, I suppose that would be for the best."

That's a smart businessman for you. He caught on quickly.

"So, what shall we do about the offering?"

It was true, I was accepting offerings from everyone I'd healed so far. Though, it wasn't like I wanted to take money from people who didn't have much to begin with; I just wanted their gratitude. It could be anything from a single radish they had in their kitchen, to a wooden good luck charm that their kid had made. One mother and child really didn't have anything to their name, so I ended up patting and rubbing up against the little girl in question as payment, calling it "healing for the soul." I ended up leaving *them* about twenty silver coins at the end of that particular trip. This was also a form of preparation on my part, for if I ever ended up doing similar services for a noble or some other wealthy person. I'd been doing this free of charge all this time, and it'd be pretty lame on my part to suddenly ask for a mound of cash for my services. That was why I decided to have people give me whatever they could that was within their means.

"Hmm, what should we do... Oh, I know!"

This may have been really good timing, actually. There was something he could get me that I thought I'd be needing soon enough.

"Do you think I could get some new clothes? More specifically, I'd like an outfit I could wear to fit in with the nobles."

My old hand-me-downs I'd taken from the baron's daughter were beginning to get a little worse for wear, I must say.

"Ha-hah! I'll devote the efforts of the entire Johann Abili Trade Company into doing it!"

"No no, you don't have to go that far!"

I ended up having my measurements taken by the servant after being moved to another room.

"I'm counting on you, Ameri!"

"Yes, sir! Even if it costs my life!"

C'mon, guys, I just said you don't have to go that far...

Afterward, the merchant went back to the way he talked with me back when he'd given me a ride on his cart, thank goodness. *I guess I should get to remembering his name, huh. Let's see... Johann, I think it was.*

Chapter 7:
An Angel

It'd been two weeks since I visited Johann. Achille had been acting weird ever since this morning, stealing glances at me before quickly looking away and breathing heavy sighs.

Hold up... Has he finally fallen for my womanly charms?

And no, that wasn't just me overthinking things! In fact, how *couldn't* I think that? You'd have to be blind not to notice how suspicious he was acting.

Everyone at the workshop kept praising my cooking, and I understood why they lived the messy lifestyles they did. I was interested in what they were researching, so I'd often glance over their shoulders while they worked, and sometimes I even asked questions. I didn't try to scold them or be hard on them like other girls would probably do. I was probably the ideal wife for broke researchers like them—as long as they could get past that I was flat as a board and the look in my eyes could make children cry inside. Even if they thought I looked to be around twelve, it would only take around three more years until I came into my own as a woman. I didn't expect I'd get even a centimeter taller than I was now, but I was at least counting on my chest to fill out a tiny bit more. Until then, I'd just keep helping out with whatever they needed as their fiancée. That said, my physical body was fifteen years old. I thought it might be a little too early to actually start looking for a spouse now.

I wanted to travel around this world and enjoy seeing what it had to offer. Marriage could come after that.

Though Achille was an aristocrat, there was almost no chance he was going to inherit any sort of title. People like him would usually aim to be a knight or a diplomat or something, but not Achille. I really had thought he was a good guy, but I just didn't know if he was husband material. When I thought about spending the rest of my life with him, it was like… Well, it didn't sound bad carving out our own happy niche in the world, setting up our own little workshop and having a bunch of kids, but there was still so much I wanted to do…

"Hey, Kaoru… You got a second?"

"Y-Yes!"

It's happening!

"There's actually something I wanted to ask you…"

"Yes…?"

Achille paused, thinking over his next words.

"Kaoru… Would you, um… Would you be my fiancée?"

I knew it!!!

Behind us, Alban and Brian dropped the tools they were holding.

Wait, you guys too? Am I finally at that point in my life where I'm popular with all the boys?!

"F-For just a day!"

Oh, of freakin' course!

And so, I asked for an explanation, *and* an apology.

Of course I was going to have him apologize for getting my hopes up then crushing them all in one fell swoop. It wasn't like I was expecting anything to happen, though! I was totally planning on turning him down! I was just a bit disappointed, that was all!

According to what Achille had to say, in ten days there was going to be a birthday party for Cedric, who was the oldest brother and also the heir to the family name. However, this wasn't *just* a party, but a chance for Cedric to find a potential spouse, as well. He'd apparently had himself a fiancée ever since he was a child, but she'd passed away due to illness two years ago. He'd finally managed to get over that sadness, and was ready to start looking again. Thanks to the sudden boom in girls trying to marry lower-class aristocrats that was sweeping the neighboring country, this party was supposed to be packed full of the daughters of aristocrats, affluent merchants, and even the third and fourth daughters from the families of earls and marquises.

Why is that even a trend in the first place, though...

Anyway, Achille's dad was thinking that this might be Achille's lucky break to find a third daughter of some baron to get engaged to, or maybe even the daughter of a merchant, which was why his father was being pretty strict about making sure he came to the party. The second-oldest son had already found a fiancée too.

Achille wouldn't look half-bad if he cleaned up and wore some fancier clothes, after all, and that wasn't mentioning the *huge* implications it would have for any merchant's daughter coming from a commoner's background being able to marry into the aristocracy through him. His parents had let him do what he wanted till now, but it seemed like they were beginning to get worried, and therefore he couldn't go against them and not show up for the party.

Achille was still having a blast with his research, according to the man himself, and wasn't even thinking about marriage yet. He knew he wouldn't be able to keep up his current research if he suddenly tied the knot with someone, which was where I came in apparently.

"You only have to pretend to be my fiancée at the party, please! That way I can get past this somehow!"

You kidding me?

"I'm just a commoner, though."

"And I'm not much different, being the third son of a low-ranking aristocrat. My parents wouldn't have anything to complain about if I brought you, Kaoru!"

"Psssh…"

"Please, I'm begging you! I won't complain, even if this all goes horribly wrong! Just think of it as helping a guy out!"

He kept on begging, and eventually I gave in. I did turn down his offer to get me a dress, though, and told him I had an idea of where I could find one. Achille seemed a bit doubtful, but was convinced after I swore to the Goddess herself that I wouldn't stand him up.

I also made sure to add a condition of my own: I wanted him to treat me as a girl he was trying to get close with, rather than his actual fiancée. If word spread that I was engaged to someone, it could affect my prospects down the line when I actually began looking into snagging someone to marry myself. I didn't want to be known as the girl who broke off an engagement because of something like this. That was super important to me, so there was no way I'd back down on that!

Achille looked a little bummed out when I said as much, but he said he understood. All that was left now was for him to have his family get my invitation ready. This just may have been that chance I'd been waiting for.

All right, I'm gonna get out there and make my move!

I asked Achille to give me the rundown on pretty much everything I could think of: the party we were going to, the Lyodart household (which was the family he belonged to), his brother Cedric, his servants, any encounters he'd had with viscounts; the whole shebang. The first ingredient to any good strategy was information, after all.

"Hi there. Is Johann here?"

The employee was thoroughly taken aback when Kaoru asked for the owner of the company by name.

"Do you think you could tell him that Kaoru is here to see him?"

For some reason, the worker felt like they shouldn't ignore the young girl's words and went to the back to fetch the owner. If he said to turn her away, then they would just turn her away and that would be that. Still, something inside them was saying they shouldn't make that decision themselves—and a merchant should always respect their intuitions.

"Glad to have you here, Kaoru! Come on back. Fancy some tea and snacks?"

Good, he's still talking normally with me. Whew.

The worker who showed me in seemed pretty relieved about something. If I had to guess, it was almost like they were glad their intuition was right on the money.

"I've got your dress, shoes, and everything else you'll need all ready for you. Is it almost time to put 'em to good use?"

Nice one, Johann! You've got some good intuition on ya!

"I'll be attending a viscount's party nine days from now, so I was hoping you could let me change outfits here before I go. I'd also like to request a carriage, if that would be all right."

"Just leave it to me! This sounds like it'll be fun, so I think I'll tag along as well—but in a different carriage, of course. I'll be sure to pretend like I don't know you."

Seriously?

"But what about an invitation?"

"Just who exactly do you think you're talking to? I'm the owner of a vast trading corporation who also happens to have a daughter at the perfect age to look for suitors. It's only a matter of time before they send one our way, and even if they don't take the initiative, all I have to do is say that we wish to attend and they'll send one of their stewards rushing our way to get us one. My daughter was completely healed by the angel the Goddess sent, after all. This could be a good chance to get back into mingling with high society. If we're talking about a party in nine days, it must be that birthday bash at the Lyodart household, am I right?"

Wow, he already knew... That's the owner of a huge company for you.

"Oh," Kaoru interjected, "I'll be getting my own accessories ready, by the way, so no need to worry about that."

"Huh?"

Achille von Lyodart, the third oldest son of the Lyodart household, seemed restless as he nervously scanned the party venue.

Is she here yet? No, still don't see her...

It wasn't like he doubted her, but he was uneasy about whether some sort of unforeseen trouble or accident could keep her from coming.

Cedric, the guest of honor for today's party, was already present, along with the rest of the Lyodart family. It appeared that most of the guests had already arrived, as well. This wasn't like parties back in Japan, where the host would give a speech right at the beginning. Carriages and wagons were the de facto method of transportation here, and were also the reason guests would often be late arriving to these soirées. That's why most people would chat and mingle for a certain amount of time before the hosts got into their speeches and whatnot, which was why it could be said that the party had already begun.

Right as Achille's nerves were about to reach a breaking point, a small girl showed up at the party.

Viscount Lyodart was suddenly made aware that the conversations he'd been hearing around him had died out, and the party had gone completely silent.

Did something happen...?

Not only was this a party for his oldest son, but a chance for him to find a suitable partner for himself. He couldn't let someone come in and rain on their parade.

The viscount turned his gaze to look where all the stupefied guests were focused, finding the source of the commotion to be a twelve-year-old girl. She had glossy black hair that came down to her shoulders, and a face that was quite pleasing to the eye. The look in her own eyes was a bit sharp, but that showed how strong her will was as an aristocrat. And that outfit! Words couldn't describe the beauty of that pure white dress that adorned her figure. It was enough to make anyone think she was a member of the royal family—and that wasn't even mentioning the jewels on her necklace and hair ornaments. Just how much could something like that be worth?!

No, it wasn't a simple matter of price here. There were just some things in this world that one couldn't buy, no matter how much money they managed to save, and that perfectly described the various accessories she wore.

She was still a young girl, not quite of age yet, but that only meant it was a matter of waiting a few years. She had the type of beautiful, graceful figure that would make anyone more than happy to watch her mature from as close as they could get. Her eyes seemed to reveal how intelligent and sadistic...er, strong-willed...she was, and who knew how many hundreds of gold coins her jewelry cost...

What family does she belong to? Or is she a princess from some other country attending incognito? Those eyes definitely make her seem like she would let out a high-pitched, derisive laugh, just like someone of that stature would do...

The party stayed dead silent. Everyone watched as the girl walked directly toward where Viscount Lyodart and Cedric were seated...then took a right and headed for the food corner.

The viscount's head dropped in pure shock. She'd just blown right past them all. Everyone's hearts stopped all at once when they saw her begin happily (and haphazardly) piling food onto her plate.

Her dress is going to get dirty!!!

Several maids practically flew over to her, taking the plate away from the girl and asking what she wanted so they could get it for her. Taking the now full plate back, the girl looked like she was in heaven as she dug into the food.

Sound finally returned to the once quiet party, and a swarm of boys had formed around her, ready to try to talk to the girl. However, it was basic manners not to talk with someone who was holding a plate of food, and none of them were able to approach, as she showed no signs of stopping her personal all-you-can-eat buffet.

And, boy, did the girl just keep on eating. The group of men were restless and fidgeting, each one ready to fight for the chance to talk with her first.

The girl glanced over toward the men, then finally set her plate down on the table.

N-Now's our chance!!!

Right when the boys scrambled at the chance to be the first one to talk with her—

"Thanks for inviting me, Achille!" the girl announced with a smile, staring straight at the third-oldest son of the Lyodart household.

"K-Kaoru...?" Achille barely managed to reply, his mouth agape.

What's going on here? That girl knows Achille somehow? But even though I'm curious, I can't just butt into the conversation... I have to fulfill my duty as host of the party.

Viscount Lyodart suppressed his urge to rush over to his son and begin interrogating the boy for all the details.

Cedric was dying to know what was going on, as well, but he was stuck in the same position as his father and couldn't leave his seat at the host's table. He had to stay there so they could both greet the various families and potential wives who came to see them.

Just who is that girl, and how does she know Achille??? the two thought.

"Would you be kind enough to introduce this young lady to us, Lord Achille?" the group of men surrounding Achille asked, urging him along.

It would be a cinch to approach her if she were alone, but if the girl's family, friends, or acquaintances were in attendance as well, it was an unspoken rule to have them introduce her to the men instead.

"R-Right... This is Kaoru."

There wasn't anything else he could say besides that. She couldn't say her family name, since she was only a commoner, and there wasn't any way he could tell them she was the housekeeper for his workshop. If he tried introducing her like that, when she was wearing such a dress and such jewelry, they were liable to tell him to quit screwing around.

Achille was at a loss for what to do—which was when Kaoru came to his rescue.

"My name's Kaoru, and as for my family name... Let's just keep that a secret for now, please."

Their suspicions that Kaoru was here incognito were all but confirmed by the fact that she was hiding her name. Judging by the way Achille was acting, they came to the conclusion that the two were no more than acquaintances at best, and the scramble to be the first to talk with her was on once more. They made sure not to ask about where she came from, and no one here was rude enough to ask how old a lady was, of course.

"Do you happen to have a significant other you're engaged to, Kaoru?"

"No, not yet. It's a tradition in our family for us to find a gentleman ourselves, you see."

The excitement of the group was reaching a fever pitch as they saw Kaoru gently smile at them. Their ages ranged from early to late teens, some a little older than that, and some even older. There was definitely a wide variety of men around her.

"How do you happen to know Achille?"

"He's one of the first friends I made after coming to this country, and I'm indebted to him for what he's done for me. He even eats my cooking and tells me it's delicious."

She wasn't lying.

Though the gathering hadn't thought there was anything special between Achille and the girl, they were all on high alert now that they'd heard she'd made home-cooked meals for him. She was even casual enough to address him without using any titles...

"You can cook?"

"I can. I'd say I'm pretty good at it too. When I heard they'd be serving a feast at this party, I asked Achille to let me come as well so I could compare it with my own country's dishes."

So that explains why she was digging in earlier... thought the flock around her. In reality, Kaoru just wanted to stuff her face after seeing the spread here. She'd always been raised with the idea of getting her money's worth out of all-you-can-eat buffets, after all (though it hadn't cost her a single coin to get into the party).

"W-Well, then you should come to a party at our estate as well! You could try a whole assortment of our best dishes there!"

"Well *our* head chef used to work at the royal palace, you see..."

"But in *our* family..."

What followed was an almost endless stream of invitations for Kaoru to try their various households' cooking and attend their parties.

Achille couldn't say a word to her. He was shaken after witnessing this new side of Kaoru, a girl who didn't seem like a commoner in the slightest.

189

"Ladies and gentlemen, thank you kindly for coming today!"

Viscount Lyodart's voice echoed throughout the party venue, signaling that it was time to begin formal introductions. The group surrounding Kaoru couldn't just ignore this, so they scattered and headed toward the front.

After thanking the guests for taking time out of their schedules to come to the party, the viscount touched upon some of the recent happenings in the kingdom before finally introducing the main focus of the occasion: Cedric. He also made sure to talk about his second and third sons, mentioning as well that Cedric and Achille specifically were still without their own fiancées. When he did, he sent a quick glance toward Achille and the raven-haired girl standing next to his son.

After the introductions and speeches were finished, the conversations from before started up once more, and the same gaggle of guys from before was heading back toward Kaoru. This time, however, there was an entirely new wave of people forming.

"Hey, Achille, what are they all doing?"

A flood of girls were making their way toward the viscount and Cedric, each one of them holding something in their hands.

"O-Oh, right, them. Those girls are heading over to see my brother and give him gifts. It's sort of a way of telling him to 'remember my name, please' by doing that," Achille answered back, finally able to get a word in with Kaoru, "Anyone who's already married, going to be married, or in a relationship with someone won't go though."

"Huh? You didn't tell me about that."

"That's because it doesn't have anything to do with you, right?"

Kaoru sank deep in thought after hearing that.

Hmm… All right, change of plans: I'm going up there!

"I'll just go and say hi as well then!"

"Huh? Wait, what? What are you… Wait, you can't! Don't go!"

The color quickly drained from Achille's face as he desperately tried holding me back, but I nimbly slid my arm from his grip and headed toward the host's table. I scanned the room as I did, checking to see which of the servants here matched the description of the person Achille was telling me about earlier.

By the time I made it to the front of the room, the line of girls had stretched out pretty far. It looked like everyone had the hots for the oldest son… *I wonder why?*

"Oh my, are you going to meet with Lord Cedric as well?"

After I took my place in the back of the line, the girl just in front of me spoke up. She had golden blonde pigtails done to look like two spiraling drills that curled down toward the floor, and she really gave off that "rich aristocrat girl" vibe.

"It appears you don't have anything to present him with though, doesn't it. Are you planning on greeting him empty-handed?"

It was hard to tell if she was throwing shade my way because I'd been the center of attention for all those guys earlier, or because I'd stumbled into a battlefield where all the girls here were vying for Cedric's attention.

"Oh, that's all right. No need to worry about me," I casually replied.

"Oh, is that so? By the by, I've heard girls who have dropped and broken their presents would do things such as kiss the hand of the person they met with, or give them permission to call them by a pet name in lieu of gifts," the aristocratic girl said before turning back around with a "hmph."

That was probably her giving me advice, since it looked like I didn't have anything to give Cedric.

W-Wow... She's actually a really nice girl.

Each girl in line would hand Cedric their gift and chat with him a little before switching with whoever was next. The amount of them left gradually dwindled, and it finally came to be Kaoru's turn, since she was waiting at the end of the line.

"Wait, you're..."

Cedric couldn't hide his shock at seeing the raven-haired girl from before, especially since he wasn't expecting her to come to see him.

"So you're not my little brother's girlfriend?"

"I'm a friend of Achille's. He's a very nice person."

"A nice person, huh. Haha..."

Cedric gave a feeble chuckle, feeling a bit sorry for his little brother, while Viscount Lyodart let out a strained laugh from beside him.

"Thank you very much for inviting me today. I wanted to take the chance to meet Achille's father and older brother, so I ended up in line as well."

"Speaking of my little brother," Cedric said, glancing at a very pale Achille, "it looks like he's about to keel over at any second..."

"Anyway, I didn't want to line up without having anything to give, so, without further ado..."

Though she said that, it didn't seem like the girl had anything on her, and it wasn't like she was going to give him any of the jewels laid in the accessories she wore.

"Do you think you could call Calvin here?"

"What…?"

Cedric was rendered speechless after hearing the last words he ever expected to come from the girl's mouth.

Calvin was one of the guards assigned to protecting Cedric, but also his sparring partner for training in swordplay. Cedric looked to Calvin as an older brother and a friend.

One day, Cedric had managed to break free of the vassal in charge of watching over him, and gone off rather recklessly to hunt on his own. He was eventually set upon by a graybear, and Calvin stepped in to protect him, taking on grievous wounds in the process.

Calvin lost the ability to use his left leg during the incident, which meant not only could he no longer fulfill his role of guarding Cedric, but he couldn't take on work as a soldier or hunter either. In fact, there weren't really any jobs for a man with a lame leg who only had a talent for wielding a sword. But even if he'd lost his ability to work as a swordsman, there was no way Cedric could just drive him away, especially when it was Cedric's own foolish actions that caused Calvin to lose his future in the first place. The viscount had no intention of abandoning the man who injured himself protecting a noble's son either.

Because Calvin wasn't able to freely use his leg anymore, he was kept on as a servant, instead. He'd considered retiring on his own if he couldn't be of use to the family employing him. However, he began thinking of ways he might be useful if he stayed on as a servant, like blending in with the other workers to fend off thieves and intruders in the event of a home invasion, or being a shield to protect those he served, should it come down to it. That was how he built up the determination to work as a servant instead.

To Cedric, though, it was a constant reminder of his guilt and self-loathing over what had happened. And now, this girl was telling him to call Calvin here and show everyone just how foolish he'd been.

"So..." Cedric grimaced. "You want me to call Calvin..."

"Yes, please do."

It was impossible to tell if the girl knew about the suffering Cedric had gone through. She merely stared straight at him, never breaking eye contact.

Silence...

No one was able to make a sound in the dead quiet of the room. Even Viscount Lyodart couldn't help but hold his tongue.

"Calvin, come here!" Cedric ordered, finally breaking the silence.

A servant slowly approached Cedric, dragging his left leg along as he did.

"Ladies and gentlemen!" Kaoru shouted, addressing the partygoers, "Here stands Calvin, a man who stood between Cedric and a graybear to protect his charge."

Murmurs of admiration filled the room. There weren't any nobles who hadn't heard the story of how Prince Roland used his body as a shield to save his little brother, the now current king. Hearing of someone who had done essentially the same thing deserved their respect and commendation.

"But because of his injuries, he was no longer able to fight."

Cedric's face twisted in anguish at her words, but Calvin didn't seem to pay it any mind.

Kaoru then took a wine glass that wasn't being used from the table.

"Here before you stands a man who was faithful enough to sacrifice his own body to protect the son of the man he serves, and the viscount has kept him in service to show gratitude for that loyalty. Anyone who thinks they are at all worthy enough to receive the blessing of the Goddess, please raise your right hand!"

Everyone present did so; there wasn't a single person here dense enough not to. Who knew what people would say if they didn't.

"Next, reach out and face the palms of your hands toward this glass!" Kaoru thrust the wine glass she held in her right hand into the air. "Everyone, pray for the blessing of the Goddess!"

The guests all turned their palms to the glass, going along with the mood in the room. The moment they did, a red mist began forming a few centimeters above the glass Kaoru still held. As the partygoers looked on in astonishment, the mist gradually came together to form red droplets of liquid, eventually turning into a sphere that plopped down into the wine glass with a soft, splashing noise.

"Here, Calvin," Kaoru proclaimed, her voice ringing out loud and clear throughout the room. The other guests couldn't make a sound, their ability to speak overpowered by the shock and awe that gripped them.

She held out the glass to him, but Calvin was frozen in place.

"Ah... Ahh..."

Kaoru walked over to him, taking his hand and having him take the glass. "Drink this, please."

With trembling hands, he brought the glass to his lips and downed the red liquid it held. Then...

"It's...moving... I-It's bending just like it could before..."

At first, he only tried gingerly moving it, slowly putting more and more strength into his movements as he kept testing his leg. Eventually, he even began jumping up and down on it.

After trying out moving his leg to his heart's content, he turned toward Cedric. "Haha... I can move it! Now I can accompany you to the mountains or the fields, and we can train in swordplay again... I... I can protect you, again!"

The rest of his words were overtaken by sobs as he broke down crying. Cedric ran over and embraced him, tears streaming down both their cheeks.

"Calvin! Oh, Calvin!"

Tears welled up in the eyes of those watching, who were touched by the display. Voices tinged with emotion could be heard throughout the room, spurred on after seeing the powerful bond between master and servant. They praised the benevolent Goddess of this world for the miracle they had witnessed today, offering up prayers to her.

They turned their eyes toward the raven-haired girl who acted as the messenger who'd brought about the first miracle from the Goddess in decades—but the girl was nowhere to be found.

Johann Abili was in a corner of the room at the party, wine glass in hand and basking in the emotions overflowing throughout the room.

Well, wasn't that something...

He'd already seen the effects of the girl's medicine before, but he was still surprised by the events that had transpired all the same. Not to mention the luxurious gemstones she was wearing, of a kind that not even a big-name merchant like himself was sure he could get together on such short notice.

Just who is that girl, anyway... Wait, what am I saying?! She has to be an angel sent by the Goddess, no doubt about it...

There was a single glass bottle stored inside Kaoru's Item Box. The jewel-encrusted hair ornament attached to the lid and the necklace laden with gems wrapped around her neck had already been taken away, making it look like nothing more than a cheap glass medicine bottle.

"You will have the power to create any medicine with the exact effect you imagine it to have, in any container you are thinking of."

There wasn't anyone at the viscount's party who'd been present for the miracle that had happened months ago in the royal palace. If there had been, they'd have noticed right away that this was almost the exact same thing that had happened back then. That said, anyone important enough to be able to sit with the king while he held an audience would be of too high a standing to bother themselves with attending a viscount's party. They were all getting on in years, as well, and didn't have any children who were young enough to not have been married already. On top of that, after he'd been blessed with the miraculous "Tears of the Goddess," Prince Roland had asked the temples and other aristocrats not to pry into the knight Francette and the other members of the Adan family who had spoken with the Goddess. This strict regulation over the information meant that there were very few who knew about the miracle that had taken place.

For something like this, however, it was only a matter of time before word reached the palace, the temples, and, eventually, all the citizens of the country, commoners and aristocrats alike.

Achille was slowly creeping his way to the door, taking care to make sure no one noticed him. Since Kaoru had gone and disappeared somewhere, it was guaranteed people would start barraging him with questions any second now—but he had no answers to give them.

I have to get out of here, and I have to do it now! *The door is so close! Just a little bit farther... Almost there...*

At the same time, Kaoru had already successfully made her escape from the viscount's estate, hopping into the carriage waiting for her outside and heading toward the Abili Trade Company. The driver was part of the company as well, and wouldn't spill the beans about Kaoru to anyone. They took precautions against anyone tailing them back by taking a bit of a detour before they arrived at their destination. If there really was anyone tailing them, there was a group of children on standby, ready to interfere should the need arise. There wasn't anyone pursuing the carriage, however, so, in the end, their services weren't needed.

A little while later, Achille successfully escaped from the party, as well. It was easier for him to slip out undetected since everyone still had Kaoru on their minds. There wasn't a doubt in his mind that he was going to be interrogated by his father and brother if he stayed at the mansion, and there was a chance the guests would jump in with questions of their own. The only choice left for him now was to flee to the workshop.

Since he'd left on foot, it was late in the evening by the time he made it there, and no one else was awake when he arrived. He crept inside and changed into his work clothes before laying down in a corner of the room.

Kaoru may just stay in hiding after showing off that power of hers in front of so many people, Achille thought to himself. *She may never come back here again, all because I forced her to do this for me...*

He didn't have the courage to propose to Kaoru, who was still just a child. Though he said he just needed her to pretend she was his fiancée for a day, it would be a lie to say he wasn't hoping it would only be a matter of time before it wouldn't just be an act, after he introduced her to his father. Kaoru had refused the idea in the first place because she didn't want to make it seem like she broke off an engagement, though... But if he could've just had his father meet her at the party, he was sure she wouldn't have objected to that. He believed his father would have realized it wasn't just Kaoru's looks that were amazing, but also how special she truly was, if they could have just talked.

But the truth was that Kaoru had lined up to participate in the courting ceremony instead, and even showed off her powers as a messenger of the Goddess before that huge crowd of people. Kaoru was smart, so there was no way she didn't know what the consequences were for doing something like that. She'd even kept that a secret up until then exactly because she knew what would happen...

Was she feeling sorry for Calvin after I told her about him? Was it because she liked my brother instead? Kaoru may never come back here now. At this rate, she may just disappear forever...

His mind was clouded with regret, making it all the harder to get any sleep that night.

The next morning—
I'm used to dozing off in the lab, but my body still kind of aches a little after...

As I groggily thought that to myself, a voice called out to me, just like always.

"Oh, you're awake, Achille. Your body's gonna make you regret it if you keep sleeping like that."

Kaoru greeted me with the same thing she said every time I spent the night here at the workshop, but... No, wait, what?!

"K-Kaoru?"

"What's wrong? You look like you've seen a ghost or something. Come on, I already have breakfast ready. You told me you didn't need it, since you'd be staying at your place, but then I found you sleeping here, so I had to scramble to make some for you, I'll have you know!"

There she was, same as always, like nothing had ever happened.

Huh? Huuuh? What was all that regret and despair I felt yesterday for then?

A messenger from home came to the workshop a short while after we finished breakfast. The message:*"Return home immediately."*

Yeah, figured as much...

I took Kaoru back to the storage room with me to ask her about what happened at the party yesterday. Alban and Brian were staring daggers at me when I took Kaoru's hand to lead her there, but I swear I wasn't doing anything, guys! We were just gonna talk, that was all!

From what she told me, it sounded like she took a carriage back to her friend's place and got changed there before coming back. Since I'd come back to the workshop on foot, she was already in bed by the time I got back.

But that isn't what I wanted to ask about!

"Um, Kaoru...about what happened yesterday..."

"Oh, the dress? My friend got that ready for me, too."

"No, not that! I'm talking about...you know...the thing with you healing Calvin's wounds, and that power of yours..."

"Oh, that. It's just something I got from the Goddess."

Sh-She said it so casually!

I could only fall to my knees...

The story I heard from Kaoru went a little something like this:

She'd actually come from some faraway country, and the Goddess Celestine had taken a liking to her and gave her this strange power. But for some reason, she wasn't able to stay in her country. In her own words: "I'll leave it to you to guess why."

She'd been living a normal life after coming to this particular country, but she was beginning to fret over whether using the gift she received from the Goddess to help those in need was the right thing to do. So eventually, she came to the conclusion that, "If I were to be hunted down after a few people found out about what I can do, then no one should be able to try to take me all for themselves as long as everyone knows about me." That way, she figured, no one should be able to try to capture her for their own personal use.

"Last night was when I finally had a chance to go through with it with all those nobles there, and I went ahead and took it. Sorry about that."

"Wait, so does that mean you didn't line up for the courting ceremony because you were interested in Cedric?"

"'Courting ceremony'? What's that?"

"N-no, haha...it's nothing. Haha... Hah..." A feeble laugh escaped my lips. "B-But that's not the point here! What are you planning on doing now?! This is going to blow up for sure! How am I going to explain this to my father... No, making sure you're safe should take priority here..."

As I panicked over what to do, Kaoru answered me with a calm look on her face.

"People will have a hard time believing what happened last night when they first hear about it, so I'm sure nothing is really going to happen today or tomorrow. With that many aristocrats there, though, I'm sure the big wigs should be making their move in the next few days. The rumor should have spread pretty far by then, so that should at least mean other people in power wanting to hog me for themselves shouldn't be able to do so without anyone knowing about it."

"Um...big wigs?"

"Right. Like the royal palace, or other people like that."

"..."

"Oh, you should tell your father that I'm a girl who fled her country after they tried turning me into a political tool, and we just happened to get close. You should also tell him you're the only aristocrat I trust right now in this country. It's the truth, after all. I'm sure the big wigs will come to you soon enough to try to get you to call for me, but I don't mind you telling them about me when that happens. No one would think I'd be a commoner, let alone working as a housekeeper in a place like this, so I'm sure they won't find me that easily."

"Wh-What are you getting at, Kaoru...?"

"Um... It sounds like you wanted to see me, Father?"

"Mind your tongue! You're going to tell me everything you know about that girl, and you'll do so this very instant!"

When Achille went back to his family's residence, his father was there to greet him—and was absolutely fuming. They were in his father's study, with Cedric in the room, as well.

"What do you think happened after what she did last night?! At least there was still some semblance of it being a party, since Cedric's courting ceremony came toward the end, but do you know what sort of uproar she ended up causing?! Do you know the barrage of questions I had to endure?!"

Achille shrunk back, startled by how furious his usually gentle father was.

"'What family does she belong to?' 'What's her relationship with Achille?' 'She lined up for the courting ceremony, so does that mean she's interested in Cedric?' 'What was that power she used?' 'Is she an angel sent from Celestine herself?' 'What does the Lyodart household have to do with her?' I didn't know a damn thing! There wasn't a single question I could answer, but do you think that was enough to satisfy those people after they'd worked themselves up into such a fervor? Why did you run away by yourself, Achille?!"

I mean, it's pretty obvious it was because I didn't want all those questions being pointed at me, Father...

Achille explained everything to the viscount just the way Kaoru had told him to. The viscount was overjoyed upon hearing that his son was the only person the girl trusted, but that joy was accompanied by other things he had to take into consideration, as well. This girl had earned the affection of the Goddess herself, so they'd want to stay in her good graces. If they could stay close with her, and the relationship between his son and the girl became more intimate, then eventually...

But would something like that be allowed for the family of a mere viscount? Wasn't there a chance that earls, marquises, and maybe even the royal family would swarm over the girl because they wanted her for themselves? Would the Lyodart household be able to survive as the only one the girl was close to? It wasn't just being caught up in the strife over getting the girl he was worried about, but that they could be wiped out entirely to get their family out of the picture. Even if they tried to distance themselves now out of fear, rumors of what had happened last night were probably spreading even this very second: the girl was close with Achille, had lined up to participate in the courting ceremony for Cedric, and had performed a miracle for Cedric and his servant. It was too late to back out now.

"All right, I understand. Achille, do you know where she is right now?"

"I do. No one should be able to find her for the time being."

"Good. Then if we receive a royal decree, we will follow it and act as mediators for whatever happens next. Ignore all questions and pressure from the other noble families. Until then, I want you to protect her and stay close. Be wary of people shadowing you when you go to meet with her!"

"Understood."

"Achille, I want you to tell her something from me," Cedric suddenly spoke up after quietly listening this whole time, "Tell Miss Kaoru that I happily accept her proposal of courtship, if you could."

Oh, that... You know what, I think it's time I messed with my brother a bit.

"Kaoru didn't seem to know that was the courting ceremony line, Cedric. She told me she just wanted to say hello to you and Father and heal Calvin, that's all. It was just a greeting, so she wasn't *actually* interested in that sort of relationship with you. She also said that I'm the only aristocrat in this country that she trusts!"

"Wh-What...?" Cedric stammered, dumbfounded.

It wasn't like he was a bad person or anything, but he was always so cocksure of himself that Achille wanted to knock him down a peg at least once. It was a little payback for how Cedric was always looking down on Achille as his little brother.

Before Cedric could recover and say anything back, Achille had already made a mad dash to return to the workshop.

It was only a short while later that a royal messenger from the palace came to visit the Lyodart household. Even Kaoru couldn't have imagined where the three potions she gave to Francette and the others would be used, let alone the effect they'd brought about. When word of what happened last night reached those in the palace who had borne witness to the miracle of the Goddess that had taken place months ago, they immediately sprung into action.

Achille made it back to the workshop and told Kaoru what had happened when he talked things over with his father, which came as a relief to her. Not long after, though, another message from the Lyodart house came to the workshop:

"We have received a message from the royal palace. Come back at once."

That was fast! That was way faster than I thought!

Kaoru was completely taken aback over how wrong her prediction had been. She was expecting someone from the palace to have heard the story, then laughed it off and dismissed it as nothing more than fantasy. It should've taken hearing the same reports over and over again, until word of it finally reached the king, which should've taken a few days at least. Then she thought there'd be some sort of meeting over what to do about the matter, but she definitely wasn't expecting them to do anything the same day they heard about it.

"I'll go if they call for me specifically. Make sure to confirm what day and time they'd want to see me, and tell them they don't have to send anyone to get me."

"Right, got it!"

After Achille left, Kaoru sank deep into thought. It'd be a bad idea to show up at the castle with someone from the Lyodart family, since that could be taken as a sign they were trying to keep her for themselves. The Lyodarts were only a point of contact so far, and it made sense for them to act as the mediators in this situation. That way, it would also ensure that no harm should befall them, either.

The main problem here was how this was all happening way too fast. Things might take a turn for the worse if the royal family or anyone else in power closed in on her before the rumors had spread far enough. The safest course of action would be to wait until word of what she had done reached other cliques vying for power, as well as a good portion of the population.

How were they able to react this quickly anyway? Did I just overlook something? I need to find a way to buy more time... It'd be a good idea to come up with a plan, so I don't find myself forced into being married off to royalty or the son of some other hoity-toity aristocrat family...

Kaoru never would have imagined the knight she'd given those potions to would have used them in the audience chamber of the royal palace. Even though she had a good head on her shoulders, she wasn't going to come up with the right answer anytime soon unless she had all the necessary information stored away in there beforehand.

"You got a royal summons from His Majesty himself, Kaoru. Sounds like he wants you to have an audience with him tomorrow morning."

"Got it."

By the time Achille had come back to the workshop, Kaoru was almost done putting the finishing touches on her plan.

The next morning, at the crack of dawn, by the back gates to the royal palace—

The main gates wouldn't open until a little while later, but the back entrance would open as soon as the sun came up to let in the workers delivering food, as well as servants who had the early morning shift. Only certain people were allowed in at night.

Kaoru was told that she had a royal audience "in the morning." This world didn't have any accurate way of keeping time, and it was simply out of the question to keep the king waiting. That was why it was normal for anyone told to come in the morning to arrive extremely early and spend hours on standby in a waiting room inside the castle. But even for someone who had an audience with the king, it was much too early to come and wait. The servant in charge of cleaning the waiting room wasn't even awake yet.

"Excuse me, but may I go through?" a young girl wearing what looked to be a servant's outfit called out to the guard standing watch by the gate.

"Yeah, sure. Do you have your proof of passage?"

"I don't, no…"

"Hm? Just here for a normal audience, then? You're still a little early for that. Well, whatever. Let's see your royal audience papers."

Even a commoner could request an audience with the king in this country, but only after going through a rigorous pre-screening process and a meticulous background check. Only around one of every dozen or so leaders from various villages were granted an audience, but even then it was only when it was about something important; things like a danger that threatened the continuing existence of their village, for example.

"I don't have that, either…"

"What, so you want to get inside without any sort of permission? What business do you have at the castle, anyway?"

"Well, I was hoping I could get in to see the king…"

"Without any permission?"

"That's right. No one gave me anything, after all."

The guard was dumbfounded; shocked to the core, even.

Did they drop her on her head when she was a baby or something?

But even if the look in her eyes was a little…okay, *really* harsh, she was still pretty cute.

I might be able to make this work, the guard thought to himself with a sneer on his face.

"I can't let you into the palace to meet the king if you don't have the paperwork, missy."

"B-But I have to get in!"

All right, that's the way…

"If you've got the cash, though, I think I might be able to do something about it for you…"

It should go without saying, but a simple guard didn't have the authority to do anything of the sort.

"Huh? But I don't have any money…"

Yeah, anyone could tell from just one look at you.

"All right, I guess I can throw you a bone... Think you could listen to a little favor I might have for you? The guy relieving me should be coming soon enough, so all you have to do is spend a little 'quality time' with me after my shift's finished."

"Huh? W-Wait, do you mean..." The girl placed her hands on her chest, tears forming in her eyes. "N-No, I can't do that!"

"Oh come on, it's not *that* big a deal," the guard pressed, laying it on thick as he pressured the girl, "All you gotta do is spend a little bit of time with me, and I'll get you in to meet the king!"

"No, please, forgive me! I'll never try to get into the castle again! I swear to the Goddess, I won't do anything the important nobles here say, or even the royal family!" she cried as she ran away.

"Tch. No good, huh... Ah, well, it only works once every few dozen times anyway. Man, and just when I got a cute one too!"

This happened all the time, so the guard failed to realize just how strange the girl's parting words were as she fled...

Achille had spent the night at his family's home, and arrived at the workshop later than usual. It was standard fare for people to spend the night there, so no one was too concerned about when they clocked in and started working though.

"Oh, good morning, Achille."

"Yeah, morning, Kao... Wait, WHY ARE YOU HERE?!" Achille yelped, "D-Didn't you have an audience with the king this morning?" The color was draining from his face as he stammered.

"Well, I *did* go to the castle, but the guard wouldn't let me in unless I paid him money or I went with him for some very dubious reasons. That's why I swore to the Goddess that I would never go inside the castle or listen to what any noble or the royal family had to say ever again."

And with that, Achille passed out cold, on the spot. As soon as he regained consciousness, he sprinted back to the Lyodart household, a look of frantic desperation on his face.

After the king and his cabinet ministers had finished their morning conference together, they headed to the audience chamber. They took their seats, waiting anxiously for the girl said to be the messenger of the Goddess to arrive. It had been fifty-three years since the last time the Goddess Celestine had shown herself. There had been several claims of "divine revelations" from the Holy Land of Rueda, but they were only things that were beneficial to the Holy Land and the temple of the Goddess. The Goddess herself hadn't made these announcements, as she had managed to appear in every country simultaneously in the past, but these were made by those working with the temple. No one believed these to be true revelations.

That's when two incidents had come into the picture: The first was a claim that a goddess from another world had appeared, one who also happened to be a personal friend of the Goddess Celestine. The second had only happened the other day, and was said to be centered around an angel sent down by Celestine herself. Was it really just coincidence both of them happened within the kingdom of Balmore?

Though the friend of the Goddess had appeared in a neighboring country, the incident had only involved citizens of Balmore, and even the latest incident involved a girl who was said to have come from a foreign country who had taken up residence there. Was this an omen that Celestine would descend upon the world once more? Was there going to be a new divine revelation, and could that be a prediction for some sort of great and terrible disaster?

Of course everyone would be on edge about that.

...This is taking too long.

The king had already taken his seat, and it had been several minutes since he had given the word that he was ready to receive his guest. It was unheard of to keep a king waiting like this.

The sounds of burgeoning unrest had already begun in the room by the time they received an unthinkable report:

"The girl isn't here."

Inconceivable! She'd ignored a royal summons to have an audience with the king! Even if she *were* a messenger from the Goddess, this wasn't something she could easily get away with.

The commotion in the audience chamber was only growing worse when a panicking soldier came rushing into the room.

"Your Majesty, Viscount Lyodart is requesting to meet with you immediately! He says he has urgent news regarding the girl!"

"Let him through!"

The king had a bad feeling about what was coming next...

"So what you're telling me...is that the guard watching the gate demanded the girl pay money or with her body to be let through, which is why she left without entering the castle...?"

"Yes, it appears so, Your Majesty..."

"And she also swore to the Goddess she would never enter the castle, and wouldn't listen to anything the royal family or any noble would say...?"

"Yes, Your Majesty..."

An atmosphere of shock and despair fell over the entire room.

"What is the meaning of this, Amoros?" the king pressed the supervisor in charge of handling important guests.

"W-Well, Your Majesty, I made sure to inform the person in charge of the main gates to *immediately* let any young aristocratic girl from another country through if she were to show up, and I even dispatched someone to guide her when she arrived!"

"Which is when she showed up at the back gates, and early enough that the guard hadn't been changed yet. And she showed up dressed as a commoner, no less... Why would she do something like this, Viscount Lyodart?"

The viscount relayed what his son had told him earlier.

"It seems that the girl in question, Kaoru, had left her home country long ago, and has been living as a commoner in our country. For that reason, I was told it was only natural for her to think and act as a commoner. That is why she tried entering through the gates meant for the common citizen. It seems she borrowed a dress from an acquaintance for the party we held at our household, so as not to cause a disturbance..."

"Which is why we didn't think to give her any proof to get through the gates, since we were expecting an aristocratic girl to come in her own carriage... You still made sure to inform the guards beforehand, and you even had someone ready to lead her in, so the fault does not lie with you," the king said to the supervisor. It would be cruel to blame him for this incident, and the king made sure to absolve him of any wrongdoing.

It wasn't going to be the same for whoever was in charge of the guards, though. The king ordered harsh punishment be dealt out, not only to the guard responsible for what happened, but for a thorough investigation to be opened into his superiors, the people above those superiors, and anyone else involved with security who'd given or taken bribes or committed other crimes, dealing out the same unforgiving punishment to anyone found guilty of wrongdoing. He also ordered the same strict investigation be performed on those who had influence over whom the king held audiences with.

"But now, we won't be able to call the Goddess's messenger to the castle. No one from the royal family or any of the cabinet ministers will be able to order her to do anything, and that includes myself. What do we do now…" the king spoke in agony, clutching his head in his hands.

The temple of Balmore, also more commonly known as "the temple;" there was no need to specify exactly who was being deified in the name, since it was obviously going to be the Goddess Celestine. To make a distinction between the minute differences in the religions found across the several countries, the worshipers would either call themselves Traditional, Orthodox, or Fundamental, though they all worshiped the Goddess just the same.

The highest-ranking member of the temple in the kingdom was the archbishop, Saulnier, with a variety of bishops, high priests, priests, and monks working under him. Various clergymen and women who held a lower rank than high priest worked at the local temples scattered throughout the land, with anyone ranked higher than a minister usually going to work at the temple in the royal capital. Gender didn't matter in any of these ranks, but only women were allowed to fulfill the role of "divine oracles."

Since the temple worshiped a goddess, it didn't mean that these oracles became brides of God or anything like that. Celestine took the form of a young maiden, and would sometimes speak with other young girls, which was why it was crucial for shrine maidens to be divine mediums themselves, so that they had something in common with the goddess. Anyone who married or turned twenty had to step down from their role as a medium, and anyone who made it past that point could either become a nun or priestess, or would otherwise return to secular life. However, any divine oracle who made contact with Celestine would keep their title for the rest of their life, no matter how old they became, and even if they were to marry.

Only the Cardinal and the Pope held higher positions than the archbishop, and both officials could only reside in the Holy Land of Rueda.

Balmore was on constant alert that Rueda would attempt to issue an order in the name of the Pope should something happen, and did its best to weaken the relationship between the Holy Land and the Balmore temple. Those efforts were futile for the most part, which was why the country took every effort to make the temple rank lower than the king, to keep their influence away from politics.

Once every few years to few decades, the Goddess Celestine would take the form of a young girl to hand down divine revelations for the people to avoid disaster and other dangers. It had been over fifty years since the last revelation had come, however, and there was no longer anyone in the temple who'd been present the last time the Goddess had descended. The faith of those still present had waned, and the temple became nothing more than a way for them to line their own pockets. The tendrils of depravity spread like a disease throughout the religion as a result.

The Pope of Rueda had made public other divine revelations that the Grand Temple had curated, yet they weren't faced with divine punishment. Those who were part of the temple took that to mean they wouldn't face the Goddess's wrath, so long as they propagated her name.

At present, the masses had deeper faith than the actual clergymen. Bishop Sarrazin was one such person. He'd never seen the Goddess with his own two eyes, and only saw his position in the temple as a way to support his lavish lifestyle. The image of the Goddess, a cheerful, smiling girl, was another one of the reasons Sarrazin didn't see her as something to be feared, but rather as a compassionate being.

"An angel?" Bishop Sarrazin growled. A scowl grew on his face as he listened to the high priest, who was bringing him the news that the priest had heard from a lower-ranking aristocrat.

"Y-Yes, it appears several nobles claim to have seen her perform a miracle…"

What foolishness. It was stated in the old records that the Goddess would hand down her revelations personally. There wasn't a single mention of an angel or messenger serving as her intermediary. She would appear in every country at the same time to deliver her message directly to a divine oracle or a priest, something which hadn't happened in fifty-three years. There must have been some sort of fortunate coincidence or fancy trick that the girl used to put herself in favor with all those nobles.

But wait just a second… It shouldn't matter if she was a real messenger of the Goddess or not. If all the fat cats believed her when she called herself that, it was only a matter of using that to the bishop's advantage. Even if she was found out to be an imposter, he would just end up being one of the victims tricked by the girl. He should get off scot-free so long as he said he couldn't doubt anyone who claimed to be the messenger of the Goddess. Until then, he would use her for all she was worth, to squeeze every last coin out of this fortunate coincidence.

Luckily enough for him, the news hadn't spread to the archbishop or any of the other bishops. All he had to do was be the first one to contact the girl and "take her under his wing." The lower-ranking aristocrat had also mentioned that the royal palace was looking into the whereabouts of the girl. Another stroke of luck for Sarrazin, since they had some very pious people inside the castle as well.

"Call Minister Dorn," Sarrazin ordered, wearing a vulgar sneer that no man of the cloth should ever have.

It was the day after Kaoru had been turned away from the castle gates. She was outside cleaning, right in front of the front door to the workshop, when a gaudy carriage pulled up in front of her.

The window opened, and a voice called out from the inside. "So, this is the Maillart Workshop, then?"

Welp, I've already got a bad feeling about this...

Kaoru could feel a sudden sense of déjà vu coming on. She stopped sweeping, hanging her head in exasperation.

"Yes, this is the Maillart Workshop, and I'm Kaoru." It was such a pain to go through this every time, so she just skipped right to the important part.

A man stepped down from the carriage as soon as he heard Kaoru's answer. He was overweight and pudgy, and was wearing a luxurious outfit, though it didn't appear to be anything an aristocrat would wear.

"I am Dorn, a minister of the Grand Temple. The bishop is calling for you, so you will come with me!"

Yeah, that's what I thought...

Minister Dorn was an accomplice of Sarrazin, and that Sarrazin had ordered Dorn to drag the messenger of the Goddess back with him meant that they were practically on the same wavelength over what to do with her. Dorn was absolutely expecting to get a share of the profits for supporting Sarrazin, of course. He also didn't believe that Kaoru was actually a messenger of the Goddess, which is why he didn't hold even an ounce of respect for her. Sarrazin had told him to "drag her back" instead of "lead her" or something kinder, so that should have gone without saying.

"No thanks."

"What…?"

For an instant, Dorn didn't seem to comprehend what Kaoru had just said to him. The thought of a mere commoner refusing a minister such as himself had never even crossed his mind.

As he slowly came to understand the words Kaoru had said, his face flushed red.

"Wh-What are you saying?! This is an order from a bishop! A-And you…"

"But I'm not even a citizen of this country. I don't believe I have any obligation to listen to whatever someone from a different religious sect has to say. Normally, clergymen don't go around giving people orders anyway, right?"

"Wh… Wha…" Dorn's increasing rage over what Kaoru just said robbed him of his ability to speak.

People were beginning to gather to see what all the commotion was about, right as Kaoru followed up with another verbal thrashing.

"Who *knows* what you'll try to do after dragging a girl like me into the back of your temple. I can imagine it now: 'And no one ever saw the girl again,' or, 'She ended up washed up on the riverbank, completely unrecognizable from how she looked before.' I don't want to end up as a tragic news story, thank you very much!"

217

"Y-You...little..." Face now completely red, Dorn finally managed to squeeze out those words. "Do you not fear divine retribution from angering the Goddess?!"

"Divine retribution? Do you mean..." Kaoru grinned. "Something like this?"

KABOOOM!

The sound of an explosion accompanied the roof of the carriage being blown off, and was caused by something that seemed *awfully* similar to nitroglycerin falling onto it.

"E-Eeek!"

Dorn collapsed to the ground. The driver who'd been sitting on the coach ran away as fast as he could, while the two others who'd accompanied Dorn could only stand dumbfounded behind the minister.

BAM! BAM! BAM!!!

A succession of smaller explosions erupted around Dorn as he stayed motionless on the ground.

"Just who do you think the Goddess is actually angry with? Who do you think will be facing divine retribution here, hmm?"

"E-Eeeeeeeek!!!"

Dorn scrambled to his feet, fleeing as far as his legs would take him as his attendants frantically followed after him.

And so, the rumors spread like wildfire...

"*A minister from the temple angered the Goddess by trying to kidnap her messenger, and faced divine punishment for insulting the girl.*"

"Your Majesty! The temple attempted to interfere with the messenger of the Goddess, and they were met with divine punishment!"

"Wh-What was that?!" The guard Serge had assigned to watch over Kaoru came back with an urgent report, shocking the young king.

Divine punishment?! A few hundred years ago, an entire country was annihilated when Celestine was angered... Th-This is bad!

"Wh-What do we do, Roland?!"

The king usually had things under control, but still couldn't get rid of his habit of turning to his brother for help when he felt like he was backed into a corner.

"Calm down, Serge! For now, we have to secure the messenger and put her under our protection! According to what we heard from the gatekeeper and the viscount, she said she would never enter the castle or listen to anything the *important* nobles of this country had to say, right? That's why all we have to do is find a place other than the castle, and a noble who isn't of import, and there shouldn't be any problems. And even if she says she won't listen to what they have to say, that doesn't mean we still can't talk things over with her!"

"Good one, Roland! I'll send out someone to search for a noble who isn't important in the slightest!"

"R-Right..."

You should really watch how you put that, Serge, even if you are the king... Roland thought to himself, a wry smile tugging at his lips.

"...So that's why you called for me?"

"That's right. You were the only one who came to mind when we thought about aristocrats who weren't important in the slightest."

"Oh..."

Oh? Isn't that Minister Dorn? Now that is a rare sight to see. He usually doesn't show much enthusiasm for his work, and was always involving himself with aristocrats and various large merchants. But here he is now, fervently offering prayers to the Goddess.

Archbishop Saulnier nodded to himself contentedly. He'd just happened to stop by the chapel, which was where he found Dorn diligently embracing the duties of a clergyman.

...But taking a closer look, something seemed off about Dorn. It wasn't like he was praying out of piety, but more like he was terrified of something... The fact that his eyes were completely bloodshot as well only made it obvious something wasn't right here.

"Is something the matter, Minister Dorn?"

As soon as Dorn was aware of the archbishop's presence, he clung to Saulnier's knees. "A-Archbishop! I-I've done something terrible!"

As he confessed to what had happened with the Goddess's messenger, the archbishop turned pale from shock.

"W-We must go to see her at once! Call Bishop Perrier as fast as you can!"

It was around that time that Bishop Sarrazin started wondering why Dorn was taking so long to get back, but assumed it was because the girl was taking her time getting ready to come to the temple, and so didn't concern himself too much about it...

"I'm looking for the messenger of the Goddess!" a loud voice called from the entrance to the Maillart Workshop.

Kaoru wasn't exactly a store clerk, and she'd never called herself a messenger or angel of the Goddess or anything, so she ignored the voice as she continued preparing food for everyone in the kitchen. Achille wasn't paying any attention to the voice either, since his father had made it very clear that he should ignore any sort of contact besides the messages his father relayed to him from the castle.

Bardot, the head of the workshop, ended up having to greet their guest.

"Well, would you look at that! To what do I owe the pleasure of a temple bishop visiting our workshop, sir?"

"Good day! Is the angel here?"

"Angel...?" Bardot didn't have the slightest idea what the man was talking about.

"I mean the angel sent by the Goddess, of course!"

"Well, uh...why would anyone like that be here...?"

The two were definitely not on the same page...

Bishop Perrier, the messenger Archbishop Saulnier had sent, finally recalled that he was to find someone called "Kaoru," which he promptly announced to Bardot.

"Huh? Well, if it's Kaoru you want, she's in the back...but what's with all this 'angel' business?"

Right around the time Achille was getting up to intervene before things got worse...

"Achille! Are you here?"

...Viscount Lyodart arrived in his carriage, fresh from the royal palace.

"Miss Kaoru will be coming to the Lyodart household to meet with His Majesty."

"I should think not. The messenger of the Goddess will go to the temple to meet with the archbishop."

"Are you saying you would keep His Majesty waiting?!"

221

"Who do you think is the one who always says religion and politics should have nothing to do with each other?!"

"Hmgh..."

"Mmrgh..."

The tension in the air was palpable. Neither of them could back down now. If they did, it would compromise their chances of bringing Kaoru back with them.

"Geez, you guys are noisy..." Kaoru finally, albeit reluctantly, showed her face.

"Oh, Miss Kaoru!"

"Lady Angel!"

"There's no problem if I just go ahead and meet them both, right? But I don't want to hear anything about doing this in either one of your home bases, or in a place where there aren't any people around. I'm scared to think about what would happen, so those options are definitely out. I want to meet in a place where plenty of people who don't have anything to do with this can see, and aren't under the control or influence of anyone involved. If you can promise to do exactly as I say on top of that, I would be fine meeting with both of them."

The central plaza of Grua, the royal capital of Balmore, was in a spot near the main gate of the royal castle. The Grand Temple was just opposite of it, where a statue of the Goddess could be seen by the entrance. Though it was usually a place full of tourists and bustling stalls as people strolled by, a hush had fallen over the plaza. It wasn't because there wasn't anyone around; in fact, there were enough people gathered here now to rival the turnouts for festivals and other grand events held only a few times throughout the year. There were even aristocrats there, accompanied by their own personal guards and attendants.

As of now, though, everyone was standing completely still, and a dead silence had fallen over the plaza. In the center of everyone gathered there was a stage, one that could be easily seen by all and was only a few meters high. There were tables and chairs set up on the stage, pushed together to form a triangle. It was set up just like it was going to be a debate between three separate groups.

After a short period of time had passed, about a dozen priests appeared from inside the Grand Temple. As they approached the stage, three of them broke off from the group to take their seats in the chairs provided, while the others waited nearby. After another short wait, an extravagant carriage emerged from the royal palace, surrounded by an escort of guards. As it arrived in front of the stage, its passengers disembarked. Just like the priests from the temple, the three passengers took their seats on the stage while everyone else was on standby not too far away.

There were three people from the temple in attendance: Archbishop Saulnier, Bishop Perrier, and Shaela, a divine oracle. Though she was an oracle, Shaela was quite old, considering she was in her upper sixties. Likewise, there were three people from the royal palace, as well: King Serge, his brother Roland, and Prime Minister Corneau.

Two points of the triangle had gathered, so all that was left was for someone to fill that last corner—and that last person was someone who would even keep the king waiting.

The air was thick with tension.

"Ah, sorry I'm late, guys!"

But that tension was all for naught as a young commoner girl called out from the crowd of people.

Kaoru had requested the following in order to meet with everyone: First, she would speak with the people from the royal palace and the temple all at the same time. Second, they would do so in a place that wasn't under the control or influence of either party. And third, they would speak in front of a large group of people.

Kaoru's specified venue of choice to satisfy those conditions was here in the central plaza, where they would hold a Q-and-A session that was open to the public. There were three people each in attendance from the royal palace and the temple, with Kaoru as the only one representing herself.

"Without further ado, let's get started with this hearing."

At Kaoru's signal, the discussion began.

"First and foremost, I'd like to ask everyone why they wanted to meet with a simple commoner like myself."

"Y-You're the messenger of the Goddess, so of course we would invite you to the royal palace..." Prime Minister Corneau answered, puzzled over why she would ask something when the answer seemed to be so obvious.

"But that doesn't really have anything to do with me, right? Even if I *did* go to the palace, there's nothing for us to talk about, and I don't have any business there."

"Wh..." Prime Minister Corneau was at a loss for words.

"E-Erm... Did the Goddess have any revelations or blessings to give us?" King Serge asked in Corneau's stead.

"Hm? No, not really."

"..."

The king stared back in blank amazement, both hands on the table.

Next up was Roland, taking over for his brother to ask a question.

"But from what we've heard, there were some citizens here in the capital who were saved after receiving the blessings of the Goddess…"

"Oh, right. That was only to help those who had good hearts and were suffering for no apparent reason. Even if the royal family or any other aristocrat were doing everything they could to fairly govern the country or their other territories, that's just part of their job, so it doesn't really make them 'good-hearted' or anything. Any soldier or guard injured in battle only ended up like that because they were fulfilling their duty, so it doesn't really make their suffering irrational, or mean that it happened for no reason. Neither case would call for the Goddess to step in and intervene. That's why there isn't any point in me meeting with royalty or aristocrats. I can't enter the castle, either. I swore to the Goddess I wouldn't, after I was told I had to pay with my body if I wanted to go inside."

The bomb Kaoru dropped sent shock waves rippling through the crowd.

"They told the angel to pay with her body?!" "Blasphemy! What are the nobles thinking?!"

Even Roland couldn't hide his nervousness as the people voiced their outrage.

"I mean, Celes doesn't even care all that much about what happens to people unless she *really* takes an interest in them. Unless a huge number of people were going to be killed off, a goddess like her normally wouldn't go out of her way to intervene in anyone's lives."

Roland fell into silence once he heard those words. Everyone present was also completely ignoring the fact that Kaoru was casually calling the almighty and revered Goddess by a cutesy nickname.

On the other hand, the participants from the temple were overjoyed to hear Kaoru say she wouldn't go to the palace.

"Then please, come to our humble temple!" the archbishop insisted, "As we are so close to the Goddess herself, there is no place more suitable for a messenger of the Goddess to spend their sojourn here!"

"No, I don't really have any business with the temple either."

A blank look of shock covered Archbishop Saulnier's face.

"E-Even though you may be from another country with a slightly different denomination, we all worship Celestine, do we not?! As a messenger of the Goddess, please, join us in helping the people!" Perrier desperately pleaded.

"Huh? I'm not really a follower of Celestine or anything, you know?"

"WHAAAAAAAAATTT?!"

Shouts of disbelief erupted from the plaza following the nuke Kaoru had just dropped.

"I come from a country that believes the blessings from the forest, rivers, and ocean come from the gods, and that their divine wills exist in everything. Celestine is just one of those many gods, and one who happens to be nice enough to take on a human form to offer advice directly to the people."

"Th-Then what is your relationship with the Goddess…?"

"We're just friends, that's all."

Saulnier and Perrier let their jaws drop in unison out of disbelief over what they had just heard. Shaela, on the other hand, seemed only mildly surprised by the sudden revelation.

"Oh yeah, and everyone keeps calling me an 'angel' or a 'messenger' or whatever, but I'm not really working for Celes or anything. We're equals, and two good friends at that."

At this point, everyone on the stage looked like the life had been sucked right out of them.

"Even if you try to force me to do something, Celes isn't going to allow anything like that to happen. Hell hath no fury like an angered Goddess, and it may not stop at who started it," Kaoru warned, facing the aristocrats and other clergymen who weren't on stage, "It could end up including their families, their followers, the faction they belong to, the royal capital, all other territories in Balmore, or even all the temples across the entire country. Celes isn't very detail-oriented, if you catch my drift."

The color instantly drained from all their faces when they heard that.

"If you come to me and demand that I do something for you, I can guarantee whatever you tried to ask of me is never going to happen. The gods should be respected, but you shouldn't rely on them for everything. While it's all fine and dandy to show your faith and devotion to them, you shouldn't expect them to help you, and you should never demand anything of them."

Everyone on the stage except for the oracle looked like their souls had just left their bodies through their mouths.

It didn't look like they had any more questions for me after that, so I was thinking it was just about time for me to hit the road when the oracle suddenly asked me something.

"Excuse me, but how is Lady Celestine doing?"

Is she testing me to see if I'm really friends with Celes? Judging by how old she looks, there's a chance she was an oracle the last time Celes handed down one of her revelations...

"She's got her head in the clouds."

"Hehe, I see..."

I wonder if she's talked with Celes before too? Actually, I wonder if I can just go ahead and leave now... Oh yeah, before that, there's still one other thing that's bothering me...

"Pardon me, Miss Oracle, but can I ask you something?"

"Of course. Please, ask anything on your mind."

"Um…why are Celes's boobs so big on that statue of her?"

And so, that was how the last person standing on the stage finally collapsed… Collapsed laughing, that is.

Kaoru was feeling pretty good about herself. Not only had she managed to figure out a way to keep both the temple and everyone at the castle off her back, she had so much more freedom to do whatever she wanted now. Even if she slipped up a little here and there, no one should be giving her any trouble about it from now on. She would be able to help so many more people now, and, just as importantly, she could get money for doing it. Just thinking about a peaceful life where she didn't have to worry about money had her grinning ear to ear.

The news of what happened spread outside of Balmore in almost no time at all, and that was without Kaoru knowing these countries wouldn't just sit idly by once they found out about her…

There was the Kingdom of Brancott, the country Kaoru had made her escape from. There was also the Holy Land of Rueda, whose influence had weakened in the fifty-three years since the Goddess last descended. Then there was the militaristic Aligot Empire, surrounded by nothing but ocean and mountains, who were ready to take drastic action to revitalize their steadily failing economy.

The gears of discord were creaking to life throughout this once peaceful world. Even if Kaoru weren't here, this was an outcome that would have come eventually.

But there was one thing for certain: Kaoru's existence here was only hastening the process…

Extra Story: Peaceful Days

...I think it's about time I beefed up my cooking skills.

I'd made all sorts of dishes using the ingredients I'd found here so far, but I was just about reaching my limit. I mean, the people didn't even use broth or anything like that when cooking, so everything just tasted like a big amalgamation of whatever was used to make it. It wasn't like it tasted bad or anything, though. It was actually pretty good in its own way, and they could even end up with a little broth if they boiled everything just a bit.

Still, it was nothing compared to the food you could get back in Japan.

The real nail in the coffin was the lack of seasonings. There wasn't any *katsuobushi* for flavor, and not a single one of those *niboshi* in sight. No soy sauce, no miso, not even wasabi! That's not even mentioning that spices were *stupidly* expensive here.

True, the home-cooked meals I made back when I was working as a waitress got pretty popular after they were formally added to the menu, but I had to really think outside the box to make it work. I had to make the broth for my faux udon by taking the stock I got from drying and grilling different types of fish, or boiling different types of animal bones. But that alone wasn't enough. Any *true* Japanese person always had to be on the hunt for that elusive umami flavor!

And so, I got right to it. I didn't have the slightest clue about where to get that fungus you needed to make miso and soy sauce, let alone how to use it, and I had no idea how in the world you would find wasabi here. But that was what I had my potion powers for! It was just like what that one guy said in that video that was popular a while ago:

It's not like I've been putting this off by saying I was going to do it tomorrow or anything like that, but this is definitely the time for me to *just do it*!

"Give me a potion that tastes and smells the same as soy sauce, but make it a little bit healthier, and make it appear in a soy sauce jar!"

And just like that, I had my jar of soy sauce, made exactly to order. I guess you could say it wasn't a "jar" cry from what I had back home! Haha...hahhh... Oh my goddess, that was terrible...

"Give me a small jar full of something that tastes and smells just like miso! And give me something that, oh, you know... Just gimme wasabi!"

"Wh-What *is* this?!"

"It's delicious..."

Munch, gobble, smack, snarf...

All right, they love it! That's some good, old-fashioned Japanese cooking for you.

This should make cooking up any seafood dish a snap. That said, even though we were on a peninsula, we were still far enough away from the ocean that the day I could introduce everyone to sashimi still seemed a long way away.

The five guys working at the Maillart Workshop had always given rave reviews to my cooking so far, but today's menu was on a whole different level. I'd used soy sauce as a base for the sauce that I used to cook the meat, combining that with something that was somewhat like horseradish. I'd also used a combination of soy sauce and miso to boil and grill up a few other dishes as well. I was finally able to recreate that flavor I'd been searching for all this time... It almost brought a tear to my eye.

I also managed to make miso soup and some baked miso tofu for dessert. I even made some soy-sauce-flavored rice crackers for snacks when everyone was on break in between projects. I was so happy that I didn't even think about putting together any specific menu, and just made a whole assortment of food. These weren't exactly the healthiest dishes I'd put together, and I was pretty sure I went over the budget for only making food for one meal... Oops.

"Everything's been so delicious up till now, but this is the first time I've tasted anything like this! What happened that made you put on a spread like this?"

Achille seemed so excited that I answered him honestly. "Nothing really. I just ended up making some new seasoning to try in my cooking. We used this all the time in my country, and I was finally able to recreate that flavor just now."

"Wow, that's amazing! You should open up a restaurant if you can make stuff that tastes this good."

YANK!

Bardot, Carlos, Alban, and Brian all grabbed a different part of Achille before dragging him away to the room next door. A few minutes passed before the five of them showed up again, acting like nothing had happened. Achille seemed a bit nervous as he turned toward me.

"I mean, i-it'd be *impossible* for you to get this into a restaurant! Y-You wouldn't get a single customer. Yeah…"

YANK!

Once again, Achille was dragged off into the other room. A few more minutes passed, and the five of them were back, acting like nothing had happened. Again.

"Well, I mean, yeah, it's *good*, but it's not something you should have in a restaurant. Sure, it'll probably get popular and stuff, but, uh, it's not something you should feed to customers… And, er…" Achille was so confused by this point that even he didn't seem to know what he was talking about anymore.

I could pretty much guess what sort of lecture the four of them had been giving him after they dragged him away to the other room. At first, it was probably something like, "What are we gonna do if Kaoru decides to quit her job here to open her own restaurant?!" which was why he panicked and tried to say that my cooking wasn't up to snuff. As a result, lecture number two was probably more along the lines of, "What if Kaoru loses her confidence and starts adding a whole bunch of weird seasonings instead?!" hence Achille's confusion over what he should say now.

His eyes kept flitting back and forth to me, looking pretty shook up over what to do.

…I guess I can't say that for sure though…

The next day, I tried making some of my new and improved cooking for the members of the Eyes of the Goddess.

"We should open a restaurant!"

You guys too, huh…

But hold on a second... If I rented out a little shop to open a restaurant and had the kids as my workers, labor costs wouldn't even be an issue... Wait, no, no, no! That would mean they wouldn't be able to stand on their own two feet. Even if I taught them how to cook, what would happen when I was gone and they ran out of seasoning? I knew exactly what would happen to the children if the flavor of their food suddenly got a whole lot worse, and they wouldn't have anyone around to support them.

But there was an even *bigger* problem before all that: I'd be swamped if I opened up a restaurant! I'd have to always be working, morning to night. I didn't come all the way to another world just to work myself to the bone! I was going to live a life of leisure at my own pace! I wouldn't have to worry about money, and I'd have plenty of free time to myself. I was going to spend my days living the easy life as I tried to find myself someone to tie the knot with; that was the life for me!

Heh...

Hehehehehe...

"Uh-oh, here comes Kaoru's one-man show again..."

"Shh! That just has to be her talking with the Goddess in her mind... Probably..."

"You don't even believe that yourself, Emile!"

"That look in her eyes is so evil, it just makes her seem like a bad guy who's up to no good!"

"W-Well... Yeah, I guess..."

And so, Kaoru's peaceful days continued for just a little while longer...

Afterword

Hello everyone, my name is FUNA. Thank you very much for reading through this book!

This is the second series I managed to get officially published, but it was my debut title when I first began writing light novels online. That's why this title holds a special place in my heart, but no one seemed interested in picking it up. I was afraid it was just going to disappear into the ether and that would be the end of it, but that's when I got the offer to have it published! It was even a launch title, and it was getting a manga as well! I was so happy I was wriggling around on the floor out of pure joy.

All that's left now is to hope my humble wishes come true, so please don't let this book flop so I can put out the next volume…and so it gets turned into an anime…and a movie…and a game…and a live-action Hollywood movie adaptation…

…There's nothing humble about that at all, is there?

Anyway, I'm looking forward to your support so I can get one step closer to realizing my ambitions.

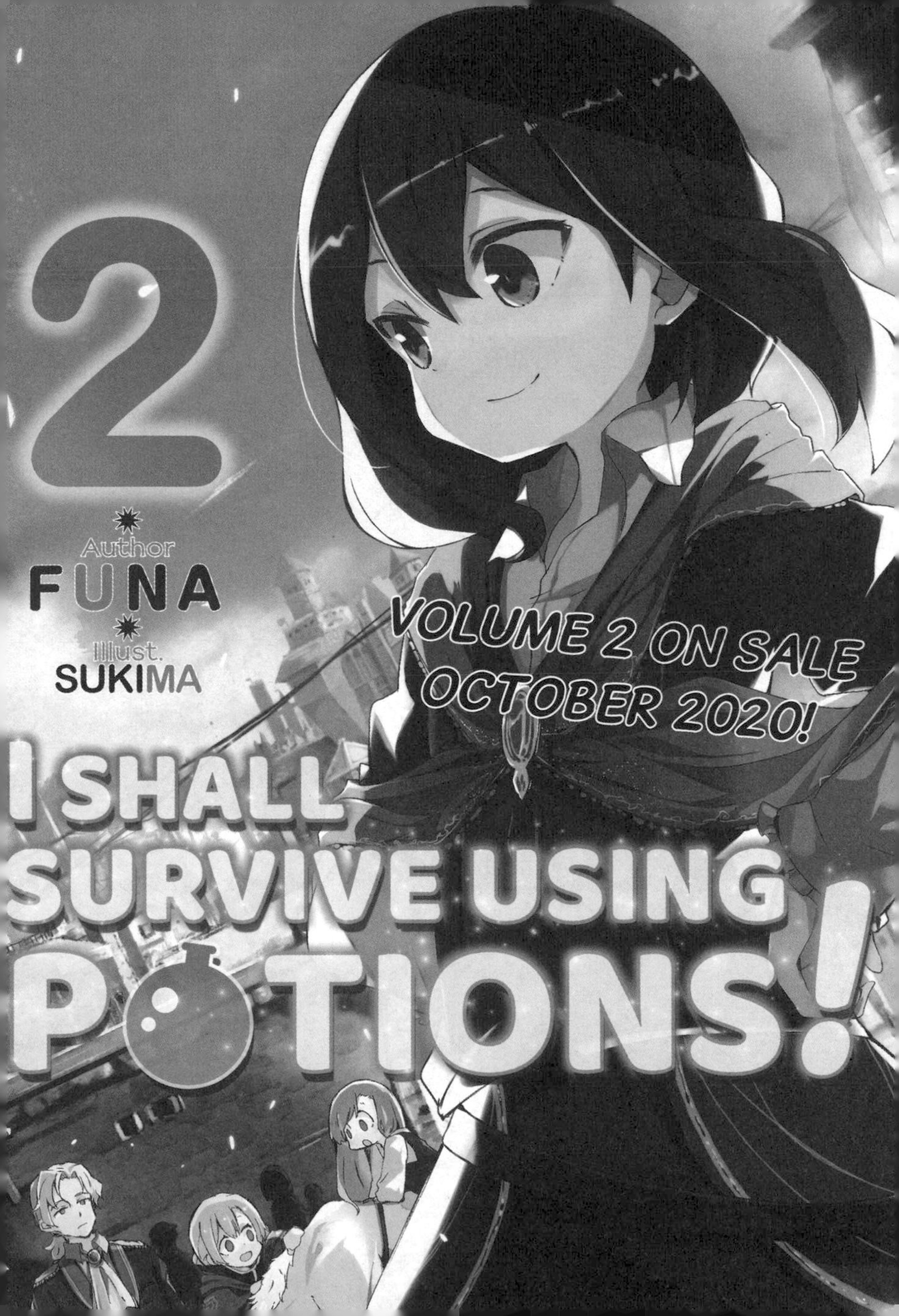
2
Author
FUNA
Illust.
SUKIMA
VOLUME 2 ON SALE
OCTOBER 2020!
I SHALL
SURVIVE USING
POTIONS!

The Magic in this Other World is Too Far Behind!

8

is Too Far Behind!

Volumes 1-8 Out Now!!

Gamei Hitsuji
illustration=Ao Nekonabe

Sakon Kaidou
Illustrator: Taiki

Infinite Dendrogram

7. The Shield of Miracles

VOLUME 7
ON SALE
NOW!

AN ARCHDEMON DILEMMA: HOW T
LOVE YOUR ELF BRIDE

6

FUMINORI TESHIM

ILL. COMTA

VOLUME 6
ON SALE
NOW!

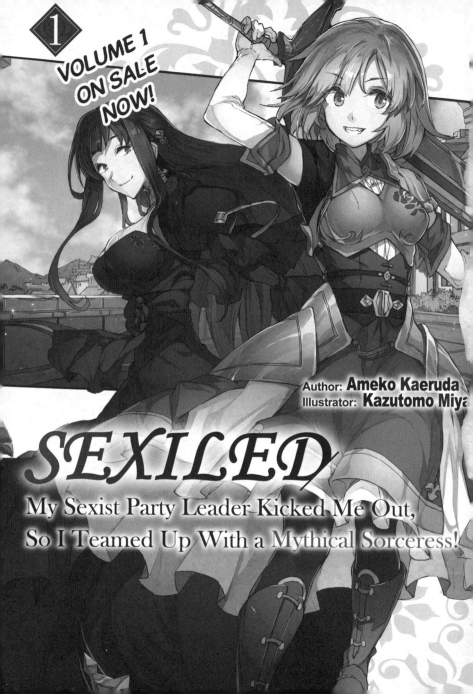

J-Novel Club Lineup

Ebook Releases Series List

Altina the Sword Princess
An Archdemon's Dilemma:
   How to Love Your Elf Bride
Arifureta Zero
Arifureta: From Commonplace
   to World's Strongest
Ascendance of a Bookworm
Beatless
Bibliophile Princess
By the Grace of the Gods
Campfire Cooking in Another World
   with My Absurd Skill
Can Someone Please Explain What's
   Going On?!
The Combat Baker and Automaton Waitress
Cooking with Wild Game
Crest of the Stars
Demon King Daimaou
Demon Lord, Retry!
Der Werwolf: The Annals of Veight
The Economics of Prophecy
The Faraway Paladin
Full Metal Panic!
The Greatest Magicmaster's Retirement Plan
Grimgar of Fantasy and Ash
Her Majesty's Swarm
The Holy Knight's Dark Road
How a Realist Hero Rebuilt the Kingdom
How NOT to Summon a Demon Lord
I Refuse to Be Your Enemy!
I Saved Too Many Girls and Caused the
   Apocalypse
I Shall Survive Using Potions!
If It's for My Daughter, I'd Even Defeat a
   Demon Lord
In Another World With My Smartphone
Infinite Dendrogram
Infinite Stratos
Invaders of the Rokujouma!?
Isekai Rebuilding Project
JK Haru is a Sex Worker in Another World
Kobold King
Kokoro Connect
Last and First Idol
Lazy Dungeon Master
The Magic in this Other World is
   Too Far Behind!
The Master of Ragnarok & Blesser of Einherjar
Middle-Aged Businessman, Arise in Another
   World!
Mixed Bathing in Another Dimension

My Next Life as a Villainess: All Routes Lead
   to Doom!
Otherside Picnic
Outbreak Company
Outer Ragna
Record of Wortenia War
Seirei Gensouki: Spirit Chronicles
Seriously Seeking Sister! Ultimate Vampire
   Princess Just Wants Little Sister; Plenty of
   Service Will Be Provided!
Sexiled: My Sexist Party Leader Kicked
   Me Out, So I Teamed Up With a Mythical
   Sorceress!
Sorcerous Stabber Orphen:
   The Wayward Journey
The Tales of Marielle Clarac
Tearmoon Empire
Teogonia
There Was No Secret Evil-Fighting
   Organization (srsly?!), So I Made One
   MYSELF!
The Underdog of the Eight Greater Tribes
The Unwanted Undead Adventurer
Welcome to Japan, Ms. Elf!
The White Cat's Revenge as Plotted from the
   Dragon King's Lap
The World's Least Interesting Master
   Swordsman

Manga Series:

A Very Fairy Apartment
An Archdemon's Dilemma:
   How to Love Your Elf Bride
Animeta!
Ascendance of a Bookworm
Cooking with Wild Game
Demon Lord, Retry!
Discommunication
The Faraway Paladin
How a Realist Hero Rebuilt the Kingdom
I Shall Survive Using Potions!
Infinite Dendrogram
The Magic in this Other World is
   Too Far Behind!
Marginal Operation
The Master of Ragnarok & Blesser of Einherjar
Seirei Gensouki: Spirit Chronicles
Sorcerous Stabber Orphen:
   The Reckless Journey
Sweet Reincarnation
The Unwanted Undead Adventurer